THE FAMILY

Charleston, SC
www.PalmettoPublishing.com

The Family
Copyright © 2021 by Adrienne Garlen

First Edition

ISBN: 978-1-68515-748-7

THE FAMILY

ADRIENNE GARLEN

CONTENTS

CHAPTER 1

THE DAY LOOKED PERFECT. THE GRASS WAS TALL, AND THE TREES were beginning to explode, filled with green leaves. Spring had finally arrived! The birds were making nests, and the mama birds were singing to their babies.

The wind blew hard at times but then became easy. It had rained the night before, and the air really smelled of dew and grass.

Vincent looked past the curtain, out into the crowd, and couldn't really see anything because of the bright spotlights that would soon be directed and shone right on him. It was his chance at the Julliard School in New York, New York.

Vincent would have to wow them with his performance on the piano. He wouldn't play Mozart or Beethoven. He wouldn't play Bach or Chopin, like some of the other students attempting to get in.

Vincent decided his best bet would be something he had written himself. As he stood offstage, he heard his name being called.

"Vincent Lorenzo?" a judge called and awaited Vincent's arrival on the stage.

Vincent walked out on stage, a beautiful man with dark, almost black, hair and blue eyes. His hair rested on his shoulders, and he smiled a timid smile. Then he rested his fingers upon the keys of the piano.

"What will you be playing for us today, son?"

Vincent cleared his throat and then said, "If you don't mind, I shall be playing a piece of my own."

"So you will not be playing a regular, classical piece?"

"No, sir, I won't," Vincent declared.

"You may proceed then," the judge said, looking a bit surprised.

Vincent inhaled, exhaled, closed his eyes, lifted his amazing fingers, and rested them upon the keys of the grand piano on center stage.

"You can never win another heart with someone else's music, Vincent," It was indeed a powerful statement.

Then in all his glory, Vincent did as he always did; he became one with the piano. Vincent's blush-colored hands led him as he played so softly at first, as if he were leaning in to love the chimes of the instrument, getting to know it, almost like he was beginning to make love to it in such magical, melodious detail.

Then, in great detail, Vincent began to make his fingers dance harmoniously above and beyond any and all notes the judges had ever heard!

Vincent had made the sweetest sounds come from the angriest chords, the most romantic tunes come from the touch of and the sounds of the keys on the piano all in this song.

From the beginning to the end, all instrumental and all on the piano, all four and a half minutes of it, it was just like Vincent had held his breath. It seemed like a race against time—like the entire world had indeed stopped to allow his hands the capability to create a rare point in time sent by God above.

It was almost as if it were a day God needed to rest, and he allowed Vincent to create a day of perfection, or that was how it felt when he was behind any piano.

It was as if God had made that piano just for him to allow him those few moments in time for amazing perfection. Even if it was only four and a half minutes, that seemed to be enough time to create a small bit of heaven and peace.

The judges were astonished. Even the janitor could hardly take his eyes off of Vincent's playing, and when he was finished, out of all the people with all the spotlights on them, the janitor, and even Vincent, there wasn't a dry eye in the house.

Vincent received a standing ovation and was then asked as he wiped his eyes, "What do you call that, Mr. Lorenzo?"

Vincent stood up and bowed to them. Then he said simply, "'My Family,' I call it 'My Family.'"

"It was nothing short of a masterpiece, exquisite."

"Miraculous, I have never heard anything like it before or since."

"Thank you," Vincent said slowly with a tear in his eye. He walked offstage and then down into the Central Park of New York.

Vincent had given the judges his room number. How he already missed the keys to that piano. If he got accepted and a scholarship, it would be amazing, something he had always dreamed of. If not, he supposed he would go back to Italy and finish playing the piano by ear and singing there.

Vincent spoke two languages and spoke them very well. English was his first, and Italian was his second. He was from Italy and had learned to sing well there, but when he had the chance at Julliard to learn so much more than he ever dreamed, his mother, Rosa, insisted there was no way he could pass this up.

Two years earlier

Vincent's father had died about two years prior, and with Vincent being the only son, he felt it his duty to look after his mother, but when the letter from Julliard came, Rosa's eyes lit up like stars, and she took Vincent into another room.

"Vincent, my precious son," she cried, "you can make magic with music. Go now to the America school, and learn there."

"I can't, Mama," he had said. "My place is with you and my sisters."

"Vincent!" She smiled. "You go now. Make your father and me very proud of you."

Vincent looked down at the letter, smiled, and then sat down, thinking of his mother. *She would have been proud of me today, so would all of my sisters. I will write them all when I hear something.*

Vincent was the oldest of his family, no longer a boy. Once his father had died, Vincent became a man. In Italy, things are very different than in America. Italian sons usually take care of their elders. Vincent was the only son. Italian men do not often have the amazing blue eyes Vincent had, but he had gotten them from his mother. Both his father and sisters had black hair and brown eyes.

Vincent was a different sort of boy. He loved and adored his father very much, and he always knew how to do a man's day as a farmer. Yet Vincent was a lot like his mother in more ways than just one. He was a dreamer. Those magical crystal-blue eyes held so much wonder in them, and he seemed to find answers in music.

Vincent's sisters, Maria, Ava, Sophia, and Gina, all were born in Italy as well. All of them looked just like their father.

Vincent was a man of nineteen now, and so all the duties of his father and his farm did fall on him. He had worked hard on that farm to clear the debt his father had owed on it and to try to make sure his mother and sisters were well taken care of.

Maria and Ava helped their mother do laundry for a woman down the street to make extra money to help with the bills. Sophia and Gina would sew and sell eggs at the mercantile. Rosa worked doing cleaning, laundry, and cooking, all the while encouraging her son to be what he wanted to be.

Vincent sat in Central Park remembering those old days where he and his sisters fought like mad all the time. Being the only boy with four sisters and the oldest, it was indeed hard. It was his job to keep the boys at bay after his father had passed, and honestly, there were quite a few.

It never mattered how hard he tried; there always seemed to be some suitor lurking around the house to seek out one of them! It had started once Maria and Ava were both out, and since there were four girls no less, Vincent's nights seemed never ending.

Vincent's father was Marco Lorenzo.

Marco was a bit stricter with his girls. He could be. Vincent, however, really couldn't be that strict, no matter how hard he tried. Marco had died suddenly at the early age of forty-two from heart failure.

One night, as Vincent had waited up for Maria, he heard the sound of preteen footsteps coming down the hall.

"Vinnie?" Gina asked.

"Why are you awake?" Vincent asked.

"I thought I heard something," Gina said. "I was right."

"It was only me, love," he said, hugging her. "Go back to bed."

Gina looked over at Vincent and took his face in her hands. "Vin, you look so tired."

"I'm fine, Gee Gee," he insisted. "Now go to bed."

"Vincent," Gina said softly, "we all know you are trying so hard to be Papa."

Vincent hung his head.

"We also all know that one son and four sisters is too much for anybody to handle," Gina said.

"Why don't you go to bed, Gina?" Vincent said.

"Papa had brothers to help him, Vincent," Gina reminded him. "You have sisters who seem to think they can run all over you anytime, day or night!"

"I am trying to make Mama and Papa proud," Vincent said.

"I know that, Vincent," Gina said softly, "but you are doing things all alone."

"What does that mean?" Vincent asked.

"Every night you either wait up until Maria gets home or Ava, and then the next day, you are exhausted, but you work on the farm anyway until the chores are through," Gina declared.

"Gina, it's only right," Vincent said.

"How is it right, Vincent?" Gina asked.

"We are the Lorenzos. We are supposed to help our people in times of need," Vincent said.

"OK, Vincent," Gina asked, "then where are your sisters in your time of need? They are sneaking off while you are not getting any rest, weak from complete exhaustion, and they are doing what they know they are not supposed to."

"Gee Gee, go to bed. I will handle this," he said as he hung his head.

"By all means, Vincent, handle it," Gina said. "Just don't wait too long. One them might end up pregnant if you do."

The door closed softly, and Vincent walked down the hall, watching Maria as she was trying very hard not to make a sound. Then he finally cleared his throat.

"Vincent!" she said. "You scared me!"

"Not too bad, I hope," he said.

"I guess not," she said. "What are you doing up?"

"I was waiting for you, Maria, just like I have been doing every single night for the past week," he said.

"Vincent!" she said. "It has not been a week."

"Are you sure, Maria?" he said. "I wait up for you so Mama won't have to see you this way. Our youngest sister knows you're coming in, at all hours of the night. You are disobeying me and dishonoring our father and family name," Vincent said.

"Disobeying *you*?" She smiled sarcastically.

"Yes," Vincent said, "I can't continue on this way, Maria. You are setting a horrible example for all the younger children. Even Gina says you walk all over me."

"What do you want me to do, Vin, huh?" Maria asked.

"I want you to go now, Maria," Vincent said. "And don't come back until you are ready to be an obedient child."

"Vincent," Maria said sharply, "you can't just throw me out! Mama will never allow such a thing!"

"That is where you are wrong, love. I am the man of this house now. I will work this farm until the debt is paid off; then I will go to America. Until then, I have given you chance after chance, and you opted out of every single one," Vincent said.

"Vincent, I have nowhere else to go," Maria said.

"Nonsense, you have our aunts, our uncles, oh, and don't forget, wherever it is you go every night," Vincent said, handing her a bag he had already packed.

"What do you think the younger girls will say?" Maria asked.

"Hopefully they shall all see this as an example," Vincent said.

"An example?" she asked.

"Yes," Vincent proclaimed. "Now go, Maria. You may return when you are ready to stop this foolishness, staying out all hours, and set a good example for the young ones."

"Vincent, Vincent, please," he remembered how Maria had cried against the door.

"Go, Maria," Vincent had said firmly, just like Papa would have, but this was a very hard decision for him to have to make. Maria was only two years and four days younger than Vincent. She had been his very first best friend, his very first playmate. This was not easy. Italians are supposed to always stick together, be there for one another, and it had been that way all of Vincent's life with his sisters and his entire family, but now, he had to think of what would be best for everyone involved.

First, he had to think of Ava. If he made an example out of Maria, maybe Ava would follow and be more obedient herself. If he didn't, then he would eventually have to kick Ava out to, and he didn't want that.

Then there was Sophia. She was between Gina and Ava, and for the most part, she did her chores, but Vincent had to try to make sure his rules were followed now.

Then there was Gina, the baby. Vincent truly did have a soft spot for all his sisters, but he really had the softest spot for Gina. She always tried to watch what he did and know how he did it. He always heard her up nights when he was awake, and she tended to worry more about her older brother than her sisters.

Lastly, there was Mama. Vincent knew in his heart of hearts Mama would go along with any decision he made if it sounded reasonable for the family, so the next morning at breakfast, Vincent gathered all of them together. He was already in his farm clothes. Ava, Sophia, and Gina were also in their work clothes with Mama at the stove.

Vincent's hair was tied back, and he sat down and began to speak to his sisters.

"I have something I have to say, and I don't want you to interrupt me," he began.

Each sister just looked at him, awaiting what he would say next.

"Last night," Vincent said, as he looked down at his work pants, "Maria came in late again. It had been at least a week. She was stumbling around, dishonoring the family name, and disobeying me. I told her she must leave the farm for now."

"What?" Ava asked.

"Vincent," Sophia said slowly. "You can't just kick her out."

"Mama, are you hearing this?" Ava asked.

"I told her she could come back when she was ready to set forth a good example to the children and honor Mama and Papa again," Vincent said.

"Mama?" Sophia asked.

"Stop it! All of you! It has not been easy for your brother. He made a very hard decision. Do you have any idea what it must be like being the only boy in an Italian family?" Rosa said in defense of her son. "Vincent did what he had to do," she said. "Make an example out of your sister."

Each girl hung her head.

"Would you have rather he made an example out of any of you?"

They all shook their heads no, and then each went about her daily routine silently and soundly.

Vincent stood quietly outside the barn, propped up, and then he looked at Rosa.

"I am truly sorry, Mama," he said. "I felt as if I had no other choice."

"I know that, my son," Rosa said. "You are the man of the house now, and so much rests on your shoulders."

"I love Maria, but her behavior was just unacceptable. I couldn't allow it around the other children any longer or around you, my dear mother," Vincent concluded.

"No matter your decisions, Vincent, I trust you will always try and make the right ones when it comes to us," Rosa said.

Vincent would try no matter what; he would definitely try.

Vincent looked off into the early morning light. He wasn't going to get anything accomplished just standing there.

"I must get to work now," he said, and he kissed his mother on the head. "I'll see you this evening when I come in."

"All right, Vincent," she said, as she watched him carry the hay for the goats and the horses on his back to be fed.

"Well, it looks like someone forgot to milk you this morning," he said as he began to set up a stool, getting ready to milk their cow. Vincent rubbed his hands together, trying to warm them up, feeling sorry for the cow.

"How foolish I am trying to warm up my hands for a cow's tits," he said to himself as he began to milk her. "Papa would definitely say, 'Vincent, you foolish boy!'"

"I don't know about that. I think I would appreciate it if someone had warmed up their hands before they touched me," a soft and familiar voice said.

Vincent looked up. It was the most beautiful girl in the village, Isabella, also known as Bella, Rossi.

"Good morning, Bella." Vincent smiled.

"Hello, Vincent," she said, holding folded laundry in a basket.

10

"You are looking lovely as usual," Vincent declared, standing up, careful not to knock the milk over.

"Thank you, and you are looking quite handsome as well," she said.

"Will you be going into town today?" he asked as he walked toward her and picked a flower for her hair.

"I think so. I have to go to the mercantile today," she said softly.

"I have goat's milk to sell. I could walk with you if you like," Vincent said.

"I think I should like that very much." She smiled.

"I will see you in an hour," he said.

After about an hour had passed, Vincent had walked up, watching Bella walk outside. Vincent had no idea why Maria wanted to act the way she did. Did she not want a husband who respected her one day?

"Hello, Vincent," Bella said.

"Hello," he said.

"Vincent, your shirt is missing a button," Bella said, feeling bad she hadn't noticed earlier.

Vincent looked down. "It's all right, I can get Mama or one of the girls to fix it."

"Nonsense," Bella said. "I have a button that is just about that size. What would people think of me if they saw you with me, and I allowed you to look all homely? We won't leave to go to into town until I fix it. Come on in."

Vincent walked up to Bella's house and inside. He had been there before, not alone with Bella though, although he had thought about it.

"OK, I will get my sewing kit. You take off your shirt," Bella instructed.

"All right," Vincent said, taking his shirt off.

Bella turned away from him, and he handed her his shirt to mend.

Truth be told, Bella wanted to look at Vincent very badly. She tried every morning to find something to talk about, and she remembered telling her mother, Cara, that he would one day be her husband. She just had to wait patiently for him.

Bella loved to listen to Vincent's dreams. She loved to gaze into his blue eyes and adored his hair, which was dark black. Every night was a new sweet dream that consisted of Vincent. His beautiful fingers, she wondered what they must feel like. Those lips, his smile, his kiss—*One day*, Bella thought. For the time being, she would make sure she tried to make his life a little easier by listening to him.

"I heard what happened with Maria," she said softly. "I'm sorry."

"How did you know?" Vincent asked, still shirtless.

"The whole village knows now," Bella answered.

Vincent let out a deep breath. "I did what I thought was right."

"Vincent," Bella said, "I didn't mean to speak out of turn. I think you did the right thing."

"What?" he asked.

"It's not like it hasn't been hard on you since your father died. Maria had to learn, right?"

"Right," Vincent agreed and took his shirt from Bella. "Thank you for the shirt. I suppose we better get into town now."

"Yeah, I guess we better," Bella agreed. "Do you have the goat's milk?"

"No," Vincent said, "I have to keep it fairly cool. I am going to sell it first. Then I can help you carry your groceries back."

"Thank you, Vincent," Bella said.

Vincent loved the way she said his name. It wasn't shortened. It came out of her mouth so softly and perfectly, almost like a song he wanted to breath in.

Vincent started to the milk market to sell his goat milk but looked at Bella. "I will meet you back here soon, all right?"

Bella nodded and began her shopping throughout the village. She picked out fruits and flour and bananas for bread. She knew soon they would have a steer to slaughter for the winter. They already had a lot of eggs, which she had also sold at the mercantile.

Maria walked up to Bella when she spotted her without Vincent. "Bella? Can I please talk to you?"

"Maria, I don't think that is a very good idea," Bella said, trying to ignore her.

"Please! Bella, Vincent listens to you. Please tell him to let me come home," Maria pleaded.

Vincent heard Maria's cries from far off, and it angered him that she would go to such lengths as to bring Bella into their family's chaos. Bella was indeed a nice girl, and she didn't deserve to be brought into the middle of it.

"Bella, are you listening to me? I am hungry. Winter is coming. Please will you talk to Vincent?" Maria asked.

"Maria, I am sorry, but no, I will not talk to Vincent," Bella said, and Vincent stopped dead in his tracks. "If you stop by my house later, I will bake you some fresh bread this once, but I will not speak to Vincent on your behalf."

"Why not, Bella?" Maria asked.

"Because I happen to agree with him, Maria," Bella insisted.

"What?" Maria asked.

Bella pulled her over to the side. Vincent watched them both and could hear every word.

"How can I make you understand you wouldn't be hungry on these streets if you had just listened to him? He is doing everything possible to and for you, and do you respect him for it? No, you don't! You fool-headed girl! You go squandering all your money away, coming home all hours of the night. It is all over the village how you disrespect your brother! You should be ashamed of yourself! I will bake your bread, and I will give it to you this one time, but only because you are Vincent's sister, and I love him with all my heart. I don't want any living soul to go hungry, but believe me, no matter what he decides, I will always be on his side. He deserves that and so much more," Bella said under her breath.

"Bella?" Maria caught her arm.

"What is it, Maria?" Bella rolled her eyes.

"How long are you going to love my brother before you tell him?" Maria asked.

"The bread will be ready about four. I will give you a blanket also," Bella said and then turned.

Vincent waited and hid against the building so she wouldn't see him. Although Bella hadn't known it, he had heard every word. He knew he finally had a girl in this village who loved him and was pure, who respected his decisions—and not only that but had also agreed with him about his punishment of his sister.

Bella stood in the middle of the street, and Vincent came up behind her.

"Vincent!" She smiled. "You scared me."

"I'm sorry. Let me carry some of those bags. They look a bit heavy." He smiled.

"I see you got apples and flour, cinnamon, and sugar," Vincent said. "Will you be making your famous apple pie then? It is the best in the village."

"I think you may be a little bit partial." Bella smiled.

"So what if I am?" Vincent said. "I love your apple pie."

CHAPTER 2

LATER THAT AFTERNOON, THE CHORES OF THE DAY HAD CALLED to Vincent, and he had answered every one.

Bella had gone home. About four, she let the bread cool and folded the blanket with it. Maria came by a little after four, not wanting Vincent to see her at all, and knocked at the door.

Beads of sweat were forming on Bella's face as she opened the door.

"Hello," Maria said.

Bella walked over to the window and handed her the bread and blanket.

"Thank you, Bella, truly."

"Maria, I would do this for anyone," Bella said.

"But you are doing it for me," Maria replied.

"Not because I want to," Bella answered quickly. "Vincent doesn't know this, and I want to keep it that way."

"Why shouldn't I tell him?" Maria asked.

"It is like I told you before, I will always stand behind him, and the man he is, if he found out I did this, I am afraid he may never speak to me again." Bella hung her head.

"I won't say anything," she agreed.

"Good, go now. Vincent will be here any moment to pick up his apple pie I made to thank him for his help today." Bella shunned her.

Maria left out the back way. When she heard a knock on the door, it was indeed Vincent. Bella walked toward the door and then welcomed Vincent inside.

"Have you eaten yet?" she asked.

"No," he said. "Not yet."

"Well, you can't have pie until you have eaten well," Bella said, as she made a plate of roast and potatoes.

"Bella, you really don't have to," Vincent said.

"Nonsense." She smiled. "I would enjoy the company."

Vincent smiled and sat across from her. Then he began to eat. It was as good or better than Rosa's.

"How is it?" Bella asked, awaiting his response.

"It is very good." He smiled. "But I do admit I am really waiting for the pie the most."

"You are so sweet, Vincent." She smiled. "I will cut you a slice of pie as soon as you are finished."

"Thank you," he said.

Vincent looked toward Bella. He had known her for a little while now. She was beautiful with long, full black hair. She had brown eyes and light, rosy-peach skin from working outside. Bella was no stranger to hard work at all. She had lost her mother and father about three years earlier when anthrax had gone through the village.

They were some of the first to get it, and that meant they also were some of the most stubborn about going to the doctor. Bella had begged them—pleaded with them actually—and still nothing. She had tried to nurse them as best she knew how, but at the time, she had only been a young girl of sixteen. Now she was trying with everything she had to keep up selling eggs, doing other people's chores like their laundry, making dresses, and selling pies, and she tried not to have to ask for help.

When she did have to ask, she usually asked Vincent, but she tried not to ask anybody.

"Bella?" Vincent said softly.

"Vincent," she answered.

"I am going to ask you something, but I want you to be very truthful with me," Vincent said.

"Vincent, I have never lied to you, and I won't start now," she said as she began to dish out an extra-large piece of pie.

"Bella," Vincent asked seriously, "did you see Maria today?"

Bella swallowed hard. She loved Vincent, but she had seen Maria. On one hand, if she told him she saw her and had helped her, he might never speak to her again. On the other hand, she had just told him that she had never lied to him and wouldn't start now.

Bella had turned from him. She had no idea what to say.

"Bella?" Vincent said.

"Yes, Vincent, I saw her," Bella said as she began to get choked up.

"Do you want to tell me what happened?" he asked.

"Not really," Bella answered as she wiped her eyes.

"Is there a particular reason for that?" Vincent said.

"I just thought if I told you, you would be angry with me," Bella answered quietly.

"Why would you think such a thing?" Vincent asked.

"Because I did something you might not be so happy about," Bella said.

18

Vincent already knew what it was, but he did want her to tell him. He wasn't angry; it was in her personality to help everyone, especially his very own sister.

"What was it?" Vincent asked. "Bella, please look at me."

"I met her on the street today, and she wanted me to talk to you on her behalf, and I wouldn't," Bella said. "But I did tell her I would make her some bread and give her a blanket. I'm sorry, Vincent. I really am. Please forgive me!" she cried out to him. "I only helped her because she is your sister, and she needed help."

"Bella, I am not mad," Vincent assured her. "Thank you for helping her. Can I ask you what she wanted you to say?"

"Vincent..."

"Please?" Vincent asked.

"She wanted me to ask you to let her come home, and I said no matter what you said, I would always be on your side," Bella said.

"Why would you say something like that, Bella?" Vincent asked.

"Because, Vincent, no matter what your decisions right now, I am always on your side," Bella was still trying to hide the fact she loved Vincent. She assumed he would tell her if he loved her.

Vincent had heard everything Bella had said to Maria that day. In a way, he wanted to thank her for defending his honor. Nobody else had, except of course his mother. He also felt a bit betrayed by her making bread, but Bella never could turn anyone away, especially if she loved him, and the person was his sister.

Vincent had heard something very special though that day. He had heard Bella say she loved him, and that wasn't something a farm boy heard every day. He did wonder how long she had felt this way. Who knew? Maybe he could have had a wife all along and not had to put up with his sisters.

That night was the best sleep Vincent had gotten in a long while, not waiting up for Maria and worrying about where she was. He walked down the hall. It was Saturday. Everybody still had chores. The girls were just there to help. The animals didn't know it was the weekend. The cows still needed to be milked, the goats and chickens still needed to be fed, and stalls needed to be cleaned out. Farm life was all day.

On Saturday, it was Sophia's job to gather the eggs, so as she did that, Vincent milked the cow and the goats. Rosa was doing housework, and Gina's job was to clean the barn and sheep.

"Vincent?" Ava asked as she finished folding the last of the laundry.

"Ava," he returned, putting on his work gloves and carrying the square bales of hay on his back.

"Can I please go over to Anthony's?" she asked.

"What?" Vincent said, wiping sweat off his brow.

"Can I please go over to Anthony's?" she said again.

Vincent was surprised that she in fact asked at all.

"Did you do your chores?" he asked.

"Yes, the laundry is folded, the beds are all made just like you and Mama like, and the barn is even raked—and that is Gina's job," Ava said.

"When will you be back?" he asked.

"Plenty of time to help with supper," she insisted. "Can I go?"

"I suppose so," Vincent said.

Vincent was in a way happy with his decision. Ava had actually asked if she could go somewhere, instead of sneaking off to do it. It was a bit surprising. The example he had made of Maria had had an amazing effect on Ava. Vincent would have to wait and see what happened with his other sisters before he could consider it an accomplishment though.

Vincent walked into the house and saw his mother, and as he wiped his hands, he looked at Rosa.

"Did you know Ava actually asked my permission if she could go to Anthony today?" Vincent said.

"Well, it looks like someone set a very good example," Rosa said, smiling.

"I hope so, Mama," Vincent said, getting a piece of warm banana bread.

"Have you seen Sophia and Gina?" Rosa asked.

"I thought Sophia was supposed to gather the eggs, and Gina was supposed to feed the chickens and sheep," Vincent said. "I will look again."

Vincent looked outside. "Girls, are you out here?"

There was no answer from either of them, so Vincent walked behind the barn and saw them both there, Gina with a lot of blood on her hand.

"What happened, love?" Vincent said, bending down to her.

"I tripped on something in the barn. I don't know what," Gina said.

"Do you know what it was, Sophia?" Vincent said.

"No, I was doing the eggs," Sophia answered.

"Oh dear Lord!" Rosa screamed, holding her hands on her face. "Gina!"

"OK, let's go, Gina," Vincent said as he picked her up and took her inside. "It's not as bad as it looks, Mama, It just needs to be washed off. Sophia, could you get me a warm cloth?" he asked. "Gina, hold this above your head."

To Gina, he said, "I'm sorry, darling, but I have to see how much it's bleeding." He turned to Sophia. "It won't stop bleeding," Vincent said. "Please go to Bella's and ask her to bring her sewing kit."

"Vincent, no!" Gina cried.

"Gee Gee," Vincent said, "we have to do something."

Sophia ran quickly to Bella's and told her what had happened. Bella was right behind her, with her sewing kit.

"Please no, Bella!" Gina continued to cry.

"It is only until Monday, Gina, when the doctor can see you. Right now, on the weekend, I am afraid he can't," Sophia said.

"It's not so bad," Gina cried.

Bella looked up at Vincent. "Do you have any bandages?"

"Bella, she is bleeding!" Vincent yelled. "And she is not stopping!"

"Vincent, she is very scared. I don't want to begin sewing on her until I have to," Bella said.

"Bella, as the man of this house, I demand you sew her hand!" Vincent said.

"Vincent, this isn't like a button on your shirt. This is your sister's hand. We should try bandages first. Sophia, go get bandages or a sheet, anything that will stop this blood. Mama Rosa, she will be fine. Just keep it up. As for you, Vincent, there is much more risk of infection to sew it, and how dare you yell at me—in front of your sisters no less?" She frowned.

"Bella, I am being serious now!" Vincent yelled.

"Keep it up and wrapped well, Mama Rosa," Bella said softly. "Gina, don't worry, my sweet baby. I will not sew it. Keep it over your head though."

Gina smiled with relief through jagged tears. "Thank you, Bella."

"As for you, Mr. Lorenzo..." Bella stood up and looked at Vincent. "If you want to risk that child's hand being infected, you should sew it yourself."

After about an hour of having her hand bandaged, the bleeding had stopped. Rosa had kept it up, and after all day, Vincent walked outside.

Rosa walked outside with him. "What are you looking at, my dear boy?"

"I am just looking at the sky tonight, Mama," Vincent said.

"What do you see?" Rosa asked.

"It is beautiful, the colors of the sunset, before night falls—purple, pink, deep blue, and the sun's yellow dipping into the far-off, rolling over the hills," Vincent said as he propped himself up on the porch.

"Yes, one might almost call it magnificent," Rosa said.

"I suppose," Vincent said.

"You know you don't have to be demanding and assertive all the time," Rosa said.

"What?" Vincent asked.

"You can relax sometimes, Vincent." Rosa smiled.

"Mama," Vincent said.

"You are always so busy being so uptight, Vincent," Rosa said. "You are thinking of everyone except those that love you." She smiled. "You have gotten your sisters in check now; that is what Papa would have wanted. The debt on the farm is paid, thanks to all the work you and the girls are doing. America is waiting now," Rosa said gently.

"I cannot leave you here, to raise three girls alone, Mama," Vincent said.

"Vincent, you foolish boy," Rosa remarked. "Have you looked at your sisters?"

Vincent really hadn't. Ava was with Anthony for the most part, and they were looking around the village for a nice little home. Anthony had graduated the year before, and he seemed to be the person Ava wanted to spend the rest of her life with.

Sophia was already fourteen, and boys were lining up, not resting there mind you, just lining up to call on her.

"Why didn't you tell me this?" Vincent asked.

"Because, Son, they shouldn't have to ask you to do every-thing," Rosa said. "Maria was completely in the wrong, and the decision you made by her was indeed the right one, but the other girls are for the most part good listeners and workers, and Gina thinks the moon rises and sets on you whatever you say," Rosa added.

Vincent knew that about Gina. He also knew he had scolded Bella when he shouldn't have. She was right. Gina's hand wasn't like shirt to be fixed. He needed to go and make it right with her.

"Mama, I scolded Bella, and I shouldn't have," Vincent said. "What can I do to make it right again?"

"Your father once scolded me in such a way," Rosa said.

"What did you do?" Vincent asked.

"The same as Bella, I walked out, only I had little kids. Vincent you were six, Maria was four, Ava was two, and I was pregnant with Sophia."

"What did Papa do?" Vincent asked.

"What do you mean, dear boy? He came and got me. He said the house was too quiet, that he needed his wife and children, and promised the only ones of us that he would ever scold again would be the children," Rosa said slowly.

"Was that so?" Vincent asked.

"Yes," Rosa said.

"I must apologize if it takes me all night," Vincent said as he began to run to Bella's house.

"Mama?" Gina asked. "Where is Vincent going?"

"He is going to see Bella, my dear." Rosa smiled, but Gina just hung her head. She was losing her brother to the world of love.

Bella sat in her rocking chair that night and was startled at the knock on the door.

"Who's there?" she asked meekly.

"It's me, Bella." Vincent spoke softly.

Bella did not answer, but Vincent's arrival had brought her to tears. She did remember back to what he had said, demanding she sew little Gina's hand, and she knew it was not in her best interest. Finally, after her tears had fallen, she managed, "I'm very busy, Vincent. What do you want?"

"I'm sorry. I will go then," he said as he started to leave; then he remembered the words of his mother. *"Your father scolded me like that once; he came after me and said he'd never do it again. The whole village knows there is a girl that loves and adores you."*

Vincent closed his eyes and walked back up to the door. "Bella, you have to hear what I have to say."

"What is it?" she asked as she flung open the door.

"I am very sorry I scolded you today. I shouldn't have," Vincent said shamefully.

"How is Gina's hand?" she asked.

"It stopped bleeding. We are still going to keep it bandaged and take her to the doctor Monday," Vincent answered.

"Do you wanna come in?" Bella asked.

"Do you forgive me then?" Vincent asked.

"Of course I forgive you, Vincent. You just hurt me is all," Bella said.

"I promise you are the last person in this world I would ever want to hurt," Vincent said.

"Bella, I must ask you something," Vincent said, "but I need you to be truthful about it."

"Vincent, do I ever lie to you?" Bella smiled slightly. "I will be truthful."

Vincent took a deep breath, folded his hands, and sat at the table. "Bella, do you love me?"

Bella swallowed hard. This was her big chance; however, she had not expected it this way! She wanted his love in return, but she didn't think she had it. Should her answer be no, she didn't, or should she be truthful as always and tell him how she really felt?

Bella paced around the room a second and then looked back at Vincent. He was beautiful, those blue eyes and that black hair, and he was an awesome provider.

"Yes, Vincent," Bella said. "I have loved you from the first moment I ever laid eyes on you."

"That was almost five years ago," he answered.

"Yes, it was. I had sprained my ankle and broken the eggs. You saw me and helped me into the house; it was when my mother and father were still alive. I was thirteen, and you were about to turn fifteen." Bella smiled.

"I remember," Vincent said.

"I told my mother that day, as you walked out, that I would marry you one day," Bella said.

"What did she say?" Vincent asked.

"She laughed at me," Bella said. "But I was serious. I told her no matter how long it took, I would wait for you."

"Is that why you stay away from other suitors then?" Vincent asked.

"I suppose so, and also why I guess they stay away from me," Bella answered.

"What?" Vincent said.

"They all know I am waiting for you, and if I die waiting for you, so be it," Bella said.

Vincent didn't know what to say at first. The entire village knew Bella had loved him. He was the reason she was turning down other suitors, and she had just told him she would wait as long as it took for him. Vincent only saw her as a beautiful girl, but there was so much on his mind right now—his mother, his sisters, the farm, and his dream to go to America.

"Would you wait for me if I went to America to Julliard?" Vincent asked.

"America? The music school where you applied! Yes, Vincent, I would wait for you forever." Bella smiled. "Did you hear back from them?"

"They want me to come in and play for them. If I am accepted, I can get a four-year scholarship," Vincent said.

"Vincent, this is your dream. You must go. I will be here when you get back," Bella assured him.

"Promise me that, Bella," Vincent said.

"I promise you that, Vincent." Bella smiled.

That was how Vincent came to be at the Julliard School in New York. He had raised enough money to go to America and then was accepted with the amazing work of art that he simply called "My Family." Everyone loved it!

Vincent wasn't just a farm boy anymore. He was in a big city, which was loud. He wondered what Mama and the girls would think of this and especially Bella. None of them would know what to make of this place.

New York didn't really have any animals that he saw, possibly snobby dogs and dog walkers, but that was about it.

Vincent wasn't used to loud horns and honking or people screaming; it didn't sound like home at all. Everything sounded mind-blowing. He felt like a small dot in a big world where time never stopped.

Everything there was so expensive too! Things at home, like hotels, were not nearly as expensive as they were there. Maybe if he got accepted into the school, he could be in a dorm room or something. Right then, he should probably focus on getting a job and writing to his family later that night.

Dear Family,

I have arrived in New York and have been accepted into the Julliard School of Music! I received a scholarship for the next four years and will receive free tuition and room and board. I must say, New York is terribly expensive and very loud! Everywhere I turn, it seems someone is wanting something from me, but I will take into consideration my love of music and try to focus on that and also my love of performance. It does seem to soothe my soul to play the piano. I really must go for now. Give my love to everyone.

Love Always, Vincent

CHAPTER 3

VINCENT DROPPED HIS LETTER OFF THE NEXT MORNING, AND IT took over two weeks to reach his little hometown right outside of Teramo, Italy. However, the family was overjoyed once they saw a letter from Vincent was there and that he had been accepted. Gina was happy, but she still wasn't as happy as Rosa. Gina had loved Vincent and never wanted him to go off to America anyway. She said, "He will never come back if he goes."

"Of course he will," Rosa had said. "Four years is not that long."

"He will miss all of my growing up years," Gina said.

"Gina, my love, Vincent had to go and do something for himself. He did so much for us. He will return home, but allow him the chance to have his freedom and to learn," Rosa said.

Gina still wasn't happy, but she loved her mother, and she loved Vincent. Even though she missed him, she would have to realize that there was an entire world out there awaiting him.

He'll come back, Gina thought to her eleven-year-old self, gazing outside her window with a tear streaming down her face. "It may take four years, and I may be sixteen, but he'll come back."

On down the road a small way was Bella, gazing at the same moon that Gina was that night. Rosa had also read her the letter and hugged her. Bella seemed very happy about Vincent's dream to go to America but also very sad indeed. The next four years would be complete torture without seeing him every day. Without his divine voice or funny ways, it would simply be torture.

Bella had promised to wait on Vincent though, and she intended to do so, come what may. She had made a solemn promise to him and was not about to break it. Vincent was possibly the only good man left there, and Bella did not want to mess that up by sleeping with so many suitors in this town. They would all simply have to keep away. She was saving her love and her entire self for Vincent.

"Come home safe to me, Vincent, no matter how long it takes," Bella whispered.

After about a month of being there, Vincent had a job in New York and had made a couple friends.

When he had gotten there, summer had just started, so Vincent got a summer job as a lifeguard. He met Tristan, who was also a lifeguard. Both of them were going to go to Julliard beginning in the fall, and they were going to share expenses. They were not very much alike except for the fact they both adored music and were both willing and able-bodied men ready to learn.

They both saved their money. Vincent sent some home from time to time to help his family, and Tristan tried saving his for the upcoming school semester. Although they were both going to Julliard, Tristan did not get the tuition and scholarship that Vincent had. Those were only given out to a few people on occasion, and it was rare that Vincent had received them. However rare it was, Vincent considered himself blessed and was very grateful indeed.

October

Dear Family,

I hope this letter reaches you all comfortable and healthy. Are you getting the money I am sending you? I hope so. I was working as a lifeguard in the warmer months, but now, I am working in a restaurant at night. The tips are good, and after I am finished waiting tables and doing cleanup, they say I can play the piano that sits on a stage inside. I do love to do that. I am living with and sharing expenses with a friend named Tristan. He was a lifeguard as well, but now he works in retail and I at the restaurant. Although I do enjoy playing the piano, I also miss the low noise of home, and I will be glad to get back to it. Don't forget me, dear family, as I will not forget any of you. Please tell all my sisters hello, and please give everyone my love.

Vincent

"Hey, Vincent!" Tristan yelled, coming through the doorway. "What is it, Tristan?" Vincent jumped.

"You gotta get me on working at the restaurant with you, man!" Tristan yelled, pulling his shirt over his head and turning on the shower water.

"Do you have any idea how frustrating it is to try and tell people all day long they look good in pants, and then they say they came in with the pants, they tried on the shirt?" Tristan said.

"You did that again!" Vincent laughed.

"Don't laugh too hard, my friend. Get me a job with you so I can wear a uniform, and I won't have to remember all this crap every freaking day," Tristan said, going into the bathroom and slamming the door.

"I will try, my friend. I will certainly try." Vincent smiled and then shook his head as he looked at his letter.

Vincent wondered what the farm must look like without him. He wondered if everyone was well, if the weeds needed pulling up, or if the money he was sending was enough to hire it done. Vincent had also thought of the meat for this winter. What would the family do? They only had the one cow, and it was used for milking. They could always use goat's milk, he guessed, and kill the deer and have it for the winter. They had the money he was sending back home now and the rifle his papa had. Sophia was a good shot. Deer season was soon, and rabbit season was just around the corner.

What would Bella do? He hoped she was eating with his family. He was afraid she might be skin and bones when he saw her next, but he hoped not.

Vincent glanced at the letter and then outside at the moon, wondering if his family was seeing the same moon and stars as he was, or if it was all just one big dream, that they were all in bed snuggled together, and he was the only one in a huge crowded area now.

"Are you writing to your family and your sweetheart again?" Tristan asked as he came out and jumped on the bed, putting a pillowcase on his head.

"Oh, Vincent, I love you," he said in a feminine voice.

"Shut up," Vincent said. "I don't have a sweetheart."

"You mean you have nobody back home waiting for you?" Tristan said.

"There is someone," Vincent said, "but nothing ever came of it. Don't you have family?" Vincent asked.

"Nah, man, I wish I had what you had, all that family stuff; we just never had it all," Tristan said.

Vincent couldn't quite imagine life without his family or their quirks, for that matter. He couldn't really imagine life without growing up with Maria. Although she was his best friend, she was still very much like his father, stubborn and independent down to the core.

Ava had gone from the independent person she was to a more watchful one when Anthony was around. He wondered how that entire thing was going too. Vincent hoped well for Mama's sake. Sophia, as he said, was a good shot, almost as good as he was, sometimes maybe better. She really couldn't cook anything, but God gave us all our special talents. Vincent's was music.

And then of all things great and small was his Gina. Gina had followed him everywhere and had wanted to be exactly like him in every way, but it would be another three and a half years before he could get back to them.

And of course, Tristan mentioned a sweetheart. Vincent had said he didn't have one. *I really shouldn't have said that. I have a girl who said she would wait for me forever, pure as the driven snow, who will shun all suitors and wait just for me, who has told me that she did indeed love me more than anything else in the entire world, and who trusts me with everything—enough to go away from her for four years to a city this large that she has never seen or set foot in, enough to not even get a letter from me. She still loves me and goes on her word and her dreams that she will marry me one day.*

"Tristan," Vincent said, as he lay on his bed.

"What?" Tristan replied.

"I do have a sweetheart back home. I just never made it official." Vincent smiled.

"What's her name?" Tristan smiled.

"Bella," Vincent said.

"What does she look like?" Tristan asked.

"She has porcelain skin, dark brown eyes, a small nose, and a beauty mark right above her top lip," Vincent described.

"What color is her hair?" Tristan asked, trying to imagine her.

"She's from Italy; it is very dark," Vincent said.

"You kissed her yet?" Tristan asked.

"Tristan, you are disturbed," Vincent said, throwing a pillow at him.

"I am not," Tristan said. "Look, how do you know she is your sweetheart if you didn't kiss her before you left and stuff, man, Vincent."

"Because I spoke with her," Vincent said.

"You spoke with her. What does that mean?" Tristan asked.

"I asked her to wait for me, and she said she would," Vincent said.

"All I am saying, man, you better write to her, too, not just your family. She could start feeling abandoned, ignored, neglected. Hell, you never know with girls, and four years is a long time."

"Do you have a sweetheart?" Vincent asked Tristan.

"Not no more," he said. "I had one though once."

"What did she look like?" Vincent asked.

"She had brown hair and hazel eyes and a really big smile," Tristan said.

"What happened?" Vincent asked, trying not to pry.

"She was really independent, you know, really stubborn, and so am I. I like doing things my way. She liked doing things her way. We just really couldn't get along. I mean we couldn't find a balance," Tristan said. "Too bad though, she kissed good."

"You are hopeless," Vincent said.

"What?" Tristan asked. "She did."

Soon after that, the months that followed ended up being the winter months, and the family or Bella didn't hear from Vincent at all during these months until finally he wrote to them in March.

Dear Family,

I have sent money home for you all so that you will have enough for the spring when it comes time to plant the vineyards. I hope you are all doing well, as I am well. Tristan got on at the restaurant where I am also working, and we play music for tips on the weekend. Tell Mama not to worry I still make it to Mass, and sometimes Tristan even goes with me. My classes are good. Piano and the performing arts are well. We are even in a Broadway play soon called *Hamilton*. I am a bit nervous, but they say that comes with the stage fright. Have you gotten the money I sent? I know you cannot write back, but I did worry about your meat over the winter months. Please share the money with Bella, and tell her I hope she is doing well also. I will write more soon. I miss you all so very much and count the hours until I am home again. I love you with all my heart.

Vincent

"Bella, Bella!" Gina cried.

"What is it, my precious girl?" Bella asked.

"Look what came today," Gina said, almost out of breath.

"It is from Vincent. He sent more money this time, and we were told to share it with you." Gina smiled.

"A Broadway play soon called *Hamilton!*" Bella smiled. "His dreams are coming to life."

"Here is your half. Now go and start a vineyard. Mama and Sophia are already planting ours, and after work, I will come help you with yours." Gina smiled.

"Thank you, Gina." She smiled. "You have no idea how bad I needed this."

"Maybe I didn't, but my brother did." She smiled.

"Thank you, Vincent." She smiled.

Over a year had passed, and Vincent had been in several small plays and acted on Broadway, along with Tristan, and each time they had a reading, they still went back to music.

Working and recording was Vincent's first love, and he adored that more than anything. Tristan loved Broadway and loved reading the parts for it.

They had made friends wherever they went, and it seemed to be amazing. Vincent was able to send home money from Broadway plays he was in, and Tristan saved his for his school tuition when he could. They were both very excited for the other until the day Paige Murphy walked into their lives.

Both boys were sitting in acting class when out of nowhere came a blond-haired, blue-eyed girl with long eyelashes and long fingernails. She was indeed tall and had a gorgeous smile and a Barbie figure.

Neither boy could take his eyes off her—at least not that day, so when they returned to their loft apartment, they argued.

"Don't you have to work?" Vincent said.

"Ain't it your night?" Tristan asked.

"Tristan, I worked last night. I am sure you work tonight," Vincent said.

"Why do you want me to work so bad? You got a sweetheart back home. Let me have this one," Tristan argued.

"Both of you work tonight. Besides, she does too. I gave her a job as a waitress," Joe the manager said when they called in.

"Oh, well then that's settled," Vincent said.

"Good," Joe said. "Now they are waiting for you guys to wait tables then perform, so go."

Tristan picked up his guitar, and Vincent played the piano. Paige clapped when they finished.

"That was beautiful," she added. "No wonder you do so well in class."

"Thanks," they both agreed.

"Well, I better get back to work. Again, it was lovely."

"What are you doing?" Tristan glared at Vincent.

"Me?" Vincent said. "She was obviously talking to me."

"No way, man," Tristan said. "She was talking to me."

"Tristan," Vincent said, "would you please go away?"

"I won't," Tristan said. "You gotta girl, and I don't."

"Not one that looks like that," Vincent said.

"Oh, so are you gonna cheat on your little farm girl then?" Tristan asked.

"For you to be my best friend, I could kill you sometimes!" Vincent said. "Of course not!" he said. "I just won't tell her what I saw."

"Fine," Tristan said. "You didn't see anything."

"I really hate you, you know that, right?" Vincent said.

"And I hate you as well, my friend. I hope that woman is not the ruin of us both."

"Me too."

It had been almost ten months since Vincent's last letter, and the entire family was beginning to worry. The money he had sent for the vineyard in the spring was gone. Both Rosa and Bella tried hard to make the vineyards work, but there was no rain in Italy that year, so the heat ruined the vineyard and the few crops with it.

Ava had married Anthony in January and then suffered a heat stroke while pregnant, working in the fields of the hot sun of Italy. Anthony had managed a blacksmith job and came home just in time to see her lying there. Although they were able to save Ava, the baby was lost. It was a boy, the doctor had said, and when they buried him, they had named him after Ava's papa, Marco Lorenzo. Anthony and Ava mourned the death of their baby boy for a long while, but Dr. Sims said she should be able to give birth to another healthy baby.

Every day, Rosa or Bella checked the mail, looking for a letter from Vincent, and every day, they would always be disappointed. Vincent was an up-and-coming musician and actor now. He had pretty much forgotten about his home life and the ways of the farm.

All Vincent's money went to buying flowers for Paige or new clothes for himself. He and Tristan both were spoiling Paige, and she couldn't tell whose gifts she liked the best.

So she began to use them both, and being the boneheads they were, both of them fell completely underneath the spell of a woman. Tristan couldn't pay his tuition, causing him to have to sell some of his things, and Vincent had to send less money home if any at all.

Soon, Rosa became deathly ill, and being as sweet as she was meek, Gina turned to Bella.

"We must bring Vincent home. It has been over two years. It is mama's dying wish that she see him one last time," Gina said.

Bella nodded, and they used every bit of money they had to fly to New York, New York, to set out to find Vincent.

It was loud, and horns were honking everywhere. People were using bad language, and all Bella and Gina could do was look for Vincent. Bella hadn't changed very much. Gina, however, had. When Vincent had left, Gina was only eleven years old, almost twelve. Now she had just turned fifteen, and she had known hard

ADRIENNE GARLEN

work. Bella was still as beautiful as ever, brown almost black eyes, small frame—only now she was twenty years old instead of seventeen.

It was fairly warm that day in New York, but the girls had walked to the restaurant where they thought Vincent might be playing, and sure enough, there he sat at the piano, playing away one of his favorite tunes, with a blond-haired beauty right beside him.

An enormous knot swelled up in Bella's throat, and Gina just became as angry as an old wet hen. Bella almost walked out until Gina grabbed her wrist, and they sat in the back of the restaurant. Bella sat in shock at Vincent and how the girl rubbed her hand up and down his thigh and then up Tristan's thigh. Gina thought she had more respect for her brother than that. She had hoped she did; however, it didn't look that way.

When the set was finally over, Bella still crying, Gina walked up to Paige and slapped her right in her face, busting her lip!

"How dare you put your hands all over my brother like that, especially in a public place and especially with him spoken for?"

"What?" Paige said as she began to reach for a tissue.

"This is my brother," Gina said. "Hands off from now on, got it?"

Paige didn't say a word. She could have called the police, but she was too mind blown and in shock. She only stood looking at Vincent and then at Gina.

"What? Which of my sisters are you?" Vincent said, not recognizing Gina.

"I am your baby sister, and if I ever see that happening to you again, so help me, I will do it again," Gina said.

"You can't be Gina," Vincent said. "My Gina is little."

"Your Gina is not only not little anymore, she also has your Bella and your mama's dying wish to bring you home," Gina said.

"Mama is dying?" he asked as he hugged Gina and then saw Bella, sweet, innocent Bella.

"Hello, Bella," Vincent said.

"Hello, Vincent," Bella continued to cry.

"So you are Bella," Tristan asked, walking around her and then shaking his head.

"She is pretty," he said.

"Don't touch her, Tristan," Vincent warned.

"I'm not, geez," Tristan said.

"Gina," Vincent asked, "what is wrong with Mama?"

Gina began to explain about Ava and Anthony's baby, how they worked in the grape vineyards so hard, how Mama came down with a terrible fever, how they checked the mail daily for any word from Vincent, and then how what they thought was happening was that she was dying of the terrible fever and grief of not seeing him again.

"My time is not up yet; I still have over a year here," Vincent said.

"Vincent!" Gina said. "Mama has not heard from you in over two years now. You have to come home and at least see her one more time before she dies!"

"And you! Who the heck are you anyway?" Gina said.

"I'm Tristan," Tristan said slowly.

"Is it a school break?" Gina asked.

"Yes, it is," Tristan said.

"Good, then you can come home with us and try and clean up the mess Vincent made," Gina said.

"Uh..." Tristan started.

"No uhs about it. Where is your apartment? We will get your things," Gina said. "I figure the both of you working in the fields ten days should cover it. As for you, Mrs. High and Mighty, I have never met you before, and I hope I never will again, but if I do, I am smart enough to know I will slap your face again unless you keep your filthy hands off of my brother, and the next time, I will slap his face! Capisce?" Gina had been ruthless and loud, demanding and assertive, all in one.

All the people in the restaurant knew she was a fireball and knew not to mess with her. It was clear this one was Italian.

CHAPTER 4

SO MANY THINGS WENT THROUGH VINCENT'S HEAD ON THE WAY home—his mama, how she was dying and the only thing she wanted was to see her dreamer of a son. He had just wanted to make her proud in America. Now she was literally dying. What if when he got there, she was already dead? God forbid! Then he thought of precious Bella's face whenever she saw Paige with him. Bella had looked so devastated, so heartbroken, so utterly betrayed, and so lost. Vincent didn't have the words to say to her. Although Vincent hadn't been with Paige in that sense, he almost had. But Paige was a user; she only wanted to see how much she could get out of Tristan and Vincent. Bella was nothing like that at all. She was kind and respectful. Bella would be a good mother and would make a good wife someday. Paige, however, would not. Vincent was beginning to see that now. The more he looked, the more he saw. Bella sat humbly, a hard worker, calloused hands from the time she was only thirteen years old, having to take care of her mama and papa and now his. She worked in the vineyards, bringing the water, since there was no rain. In Italy, it was important to sell the wine quickly before it fermented, and although they tried, they couldn't make a go of it.

My sweet little Gina, who was eleven when I left and thought I could do no wrong definitely slapped the shit out of Paige over me! Gina was right though. I should not have allowed her hand on my inner thigh like that in a public place or anyplace. So it was only right of Gina to slap her on my behalf. I doubt I will ever see that girl again.

The ride landed, and Gina and Bella got off, leaving Tristan and Vincent.

"Man, it's hot," Tristan said.

"Wait till you get to the village," Vincent said.

"How far away is that?" Tristan asked.

"About a mile." Vincent shrugged.

"Seriously?" Tristan asked.

"You wanted family life." Vincent smiled. "Here we go."

About a mile into the village, Vincent was met with a lot of people, but he was the most worried about his mother. So he followed Bella and Gina into their house and saw Rosa as she lay on her bed.

"Mama," Gina called, "Mama, look who I have brought to see you."

"Mama." Vincent tried to smile. "Mama, it's me, Vincent."

"Vincent?" Rosa called out. "I must be dreaming."

"Mama Rosa," Bella said, "it is not a dream. Vincent is really here, and he has brought his friend Tristan."

Rosa opened her blue eyes that were a magical glass sea just like Vincent's.

"Vincent." She smiled. "You have come back to me."

"What do you need, Mama?" Vincent asked as he took her hand. "Whatever it is, I shall see it gets done."

"Vincent, always the dreamer, just like your mama." Rosa smiled. "Did you see America, my son?"

"Yes, Mama, I saw parts of it," Vincent said.

"Was it beautiful?" She smiled.

"There is no place like home, Mama," Vincent said. "Get some rest, OK? I will be here when you wake up."

Vincent walked outside and looked at the farm, and Ava followed him shortly after. The fields had grown over. It looked like years since they had even seen a plow.

"This place looks like the land that time forgot," Ava said, remembering the heat and the loss of the baby. Vincent just stayed silent.

"Anthony tried to make do, work during the morning for people as a blacksmith, sometimes at night for the extra pay; then during the afternoon, he would always work hard in the fields, but even between all four of us in this heat and dry weather, we couldn't make a go of it."

"I'm sorry, Ava. I should have been here to take care of it myself," Vincent said, looking out at the fields, once a beautiful green but now completely dried up.

"Vincent, you can't take the blame. A man can't take blame for weather," Ava said.

"If I had been here, you wouldn't have been working in the fields. You may be a mother right now, and Anthony wouldn't have had to mourn the death of his firstborn son either then," Vincent reasoned.

Ava hung her head. Vincent had been right. What if he had been here? What if he had worked the fields instead of Ava? He might be an uncle now, or it might all be just a dream. What if he had never actually left? If he had stayed and worked the farm, instead of going to America?

"Vincent," Ava said softly, "we did need you, but nobody blames you."

"Gina does." Vincent turned from Ava. "Gina blames me for it all, and I can't blame her, after what she saw, what I did."

"Gina is exactly like her big brother," Ava announced. "She is hardheaded and just as stubborn as a mule, but at the end of a long day, she tries to make peace with the world. She don't always succeed when it comes to you, Vincent, and she has been known to fight over you from time to time." Ava smiled. "You know, slap a few faces here and there and sometimes even draw blood, always ending the conversation with if you ever talk about my brother again or my brother this or that. She means well, as we all do. Gina just has the most assertive way of showing it," Ava continued to smile, a trait she had inherited from Rosa.

Tristan walked out on the porch. "That youngest sister of yours is a spitfire. Were you once like that, Vincent?" Tristan asked.

"Not really," Vincent said.

"Vincent was always a dreamer," Ava said. "Go make things right with Gina. I will show Tristan where he can sleep while he is here."

Gina sat looking at Rosa. Rosa was asleep again and was weak. Vincent walked in and looked directly at his mother and sister. Gina turned from him as if she had nothing at all to say, and Vincent just stared at Rosa, remembering back to when he was little and things were exactly how he could have imagined. One boy and four girls. Papa was still here, Mama was healthy, and everyone was alive and well—before everybody grew up and everything got so messed up.

"You know, every time Mama used to fall asleep, I would be afraid she would never, ever wake up again because all she used to cry out for was to see you one more time. And now that she has, I am not scared anymore that she won't wake up. I'm just glad you're here, that she can wake up to," Gina said slowly.

"You know you're not really the Gina I remember," Vincent said.

"What?" she asked.

"You expect so much more of me than what I am," Vincent said.

"No, Vincent, I just had way higher standards for you in my mind is all."

"Ava says you have been in many fights over me," Vincent said. "Is that true?"

"Of course it's true, dummy," Gina snarled. "When you left, somebody had to defend your honor around here!"

"My honor?" Vincent said wisely.

"Yeah wise guy," Gina said. "The first harsh word I heard about you, I slapped their face, the same with Bella."

"What about Bella?"

"Bella waited a long time for you, too long if you ask me, but because she waited and wouldn't go near anyone else, I fought for her too, just like she was your very own special doll. She spent every last penny she had to go to America to get you and bring you back to Mama. Every single cent just to find you with blondie over there, hands all up on your leg. Disgusting, Vincent."

"I really am sorry about that, Gina," Vincent said.

"No, Vincent, you're not sorry. See my brother was a man, a real man. He would have been sorry about it. You're sorry you got caught; there is a difference," Gina stated.

"I never meant to hurt you or Bella," Vincent said.

"Then maybe you should have thought of that before you let Miss Blond Bombshell touch all over you and your buddy," Gina explained.

"Gina, that is quite enough," Vincent said.

"No, Vincent, it isn't. See, you're not the head of this house anymore. You don't live here. You don't know the goings on here, and I doubt you care. Bella loved you. She probably still does. I don't know, but if I were her, I wouldn't after what I saw. Bella trusted you, and you let her down. You let all of us down. You are the one who changed, Vincent, not us." Gina marched out.

Things would never be the same between Vincent and Gina. Gina had seen too much now. Nothing could ever be as he hoped it would one day between them. Even though he had said he was sorry to Gina, he supposed she was right; he wouldn't have been sorry if he hadn't gotten caught, and who knows? The girl with the blond hair might still have her hand on him or Tristan if Gina and Bella had never shown up.

There is only one other person I can make this right with, who might possibly forgive me, and that is Bella. I shall go to her and speak with her in the morning. Amazingly enough, maybe she will hear me out.

The next morning, a knock came on Bella's door, and she had just finished baking banana bread, so when she saw it was Vincent, she asked if he wanted to come in.

"It smells very good," Vincent said.

"Thank you," she replied, not knowing what to say about what she had seen the day before.

"Bella?" he said softly.

"Vincent," she managed to say.

"I shouldn't have allowed that girl to have her hands on me, and I know that now. I am sorry the whole thing happened, not just sorry I got caught," Vincent said.

Bella slowly hung her head and then lifted it back up again. "I forgive you, Vincent."

"What?" he asked, looking around at her.

"I forgive you, Vincent," Bella said, as she walked a little closer toward him.

"Our village is small, and there are not a lot of men and women to choose from. Some are even chosen for us. There are not many men and women left anymore that will marry and have a family, but one day, Vincent Lorenzo, I will marry you." Bella was a beautiful, innocent girl of twenty. "I'll bet America is huge, and there are women everywhere, some with dark hair, red lips, blond hair, auburn hair. Am I right?"

"You are right, my dear Bella," Vincent said. "But the one thing America did not have was you and your virtue. A million other women might have come and gone, but one thing is still inside my head."

"What is that?" Bella asked.

"Your honesty, when I asked you if you loved me, you said yes; your quality, I never have to question your ability to do anything, because I know you are the best at everything you do; your virginity, I never question if it is still there because I know it is. Your love for me will never die. You are the missing piece to my troubled soul, Bella," Vincent said softly.

"I will always love you, Vincent, and always be ready to work hard for you and our family and your family once we have one. As for now, it was a shock to me; however, so was New York, very different than what I am used to. I suppose if I had been at the piano, after three and a half years with two men, and you had walked in, you may have been very upset too." She smiled.

"I don't even want to think of that," Vincent said.

"Bella." Vincent stood up. "Would you marry me while I am here?"

"Yes," she whispered. "I will marry you and be your wife."

Vincent kissed her hand and then said, "It is settled then. We shall marry this weekend."

Bella smiled and nodded.

Everyone was buzzing about Vincent marrying Bella! Bella had stored away her mother's own wedding dress, and she and Ava would make alterations for it. Finally, it was going to happen. Everything would go just as scheduled.

When Vincent had told Tristan he was going to be getting married that weekend, Tristan had said, "That pretty little girl is gonna marry you?"

"Yes, and you are to be my best man," Vincent said.

"OK, man," Tristan said, "But first we gotta help Anthony get some of these weeds up."

"You're right. I just want to share the news with Mama first. I think it will lift her spirits a bit," Vincent said as he went into the house, still in his work clothes and boots. He knocked on the door. There was no answer. He knocked again and still nothing. This time, he opened the door to find a sheet over his mother's head and his sisters all around the bed crying, even Maria.

"Vincent, wait!" Bella called as he ran out.

"I'll go," Tristan said.

Vincent ran to the barn and began sheering the sheep.

"Hey, man," Tristan said, "I am really sorry about your ma."

"It's all right," Vincent answered. "She is with my father now."

"Yeah, but it ain't easy when you lose your ma, or it wasn't for me anyway," Tristan said softly.

"You lost your mother?" Vincent asked.

"Yeah, about four years ago. It was pretty rough. I was a real mama's boy too. I loved her so much, and then outta nowhere, she just died on me. I was about fifteen then. I never really wanted to go live with my pop, but I kinda had to. I couldn't live alone." Tristan spoke more softly than normal.

"You didn't have any other family?" Vincent asked.

"Nah, you're the closest thing I got to a brother," Tristan said.

"Thanks." Vincent smiled. "I just wanted her to see my wedding day. I thought if she saw that, maybe she could have been happy for me and Bella. Mama always wanted me and Bella together, so I thought, or I hoped, that maybe if she could just see us together, it might lift her spirits some."

"Man, she loved Bella like her own. Everybody loves Bella. Your mama was just glad she got to see you again," Tristan said. Then they both started toward the house.

It was Wednesday. Vincent planned on his wedding to Bella being on Saturday. Even with Rosa's passing, there was still a lot to do.

"Anthony?" Bella asked softly one night after everyone had gone to bed.

"Yeah, Bella," Anthony looked back at her.

"I was wondering if Ava says it's OK, and you don't mind at all..." Bella started.

"What is it, Bella?" He shrugged.

"Would you give me away this Saturday, please?" Bella asked.

"Yes, yes, I will," Anthony smiled.

It made him feel honored and happy that Bella had asked him. He didn't feel like an outsider anymore but a part of a huge family that was accepting Bella into the heart of it. He knew she didn't have a father or father-in-law, and her husband was going to be Vincent, so he would gladly accept her into their family.

CHAPTER 5

FRIDAY NIGHT, AS TRISTAN AND VINCENT BEGAN TO PILE HAY IN the barn for Tristan to sleep, they both seemed a little bit anxious, neither one wanting to admit what the problem was to the other.

"Well," Tristan finally said, "tomorrow's the big day, a married man!"

"Yeah." Vincent nodded. "A married man."

"So, how come you don't look happy?" Tristan asked slowly.

"I am happy, my friend." Vincent nodded. "I truly am."

Vincent held on to a nearby rake, not wanting to go into the house but not wanting to leave Tristan either.

"Something is wrong, Vincent," Tristan said. "What is it?"

"Can we talk?" Vincent asked.

"OK." Tristan shrugged as he lay down on his bed of soft hay, and Vincent sat against the cow stool.

"The first time I ever saw Bella, I had just milked our cow, and she had fallen and sprained her ankle. I went to help her take her milk in the house. From that day on, almost every day after that, she stopped by and talked to me while I was milking our cow." Vincent smiled.

"Bella's a real catch, man. She's pretty and what every guy wants, you know? She can cook and stuff, works hard, and the absolute best part about her is that she loves you and has waited for you this whole time. Not many girls would do that anymore," Tristan replied.

Vincent smiled to himself. That was true. So many women were not chaste anymore, and Bella was one of the purest women he knew.

Tristan looked over at Vincent. "Vincent," he asked, "what is still bothering you?"

"I need to ask some questions, but I am afraid they may be a little embarrassing for us both."

"I told you, you're the closest thing to a brother I will ever have. If we couldn't talk in New York, we may as well in Italy," Tristan said. "Shoot."

"Have you ever been with a girl, Tristan?" Vincent asked, looking directly at Tristan.

"Damn, you went right to it, didn't you?" Tristan asked.

"Uh." Tristan cleared his throat. "Yeah, man, I have been with one, but that's all."

"The girl you said was a good kisser?" Vincent asked.

"Yeah, that was the one," Tristan answered.

"I have never been with a girl," Vincent responded.

"You think I didn't know that? I thought you were gay when we first met for over a year!" Tristan laughed.

Vincent shook his head. "I was taught to respect women. I came close to kissing a girl once, Paige."

"You did not!" Tristan answered. "She loved our music and our acting, not us."

"Tell me, O wise one, what am I supposed to do?" Vincent asked.

"What? Your papa never had this talk with you?" Tristan asked in disbelief.

"I told you Papa died when I was young, and I was the oldest; I couldn't really talk to Mama. She was a woman. Why not my best friend?" Vincent lay down on the hay.

Tristan's face was red, and he was embarrassed, but he could see his friend needed him, so he was there to help.

"Well, it's your first time, so it probably won't last very long." Tristan scratched his head.

"Why not?" Vincent shrugged.

"I don't know, man. The first time usually don't; that's all."

"Oh."

"I mean, that's OK and everything. It's normal," Tristan explained. "Uh, Bella is kinda petite, you know, so she may bleed the first few times."

"Bleed?" Vincent said. "I don't want to hurt her."

"It's all right, man. It happens to the best of us. Lots of girls, most girls, bleed the first time. They can't help it. Just tell her if it hurts too bad and she wants you to stop or something to just say so. They like it when guys go slow, stuff like that, and to be touched. Just don't go too fast for her the first time. It may be awkward or something. Then she may be scared every time. You definitely don't want that."

"Why do they bleed?" Vincent asked.

"I dunno. It breaks something. I forget what it's called, something important though," Tristan declared.

Vincent frowned and looked as if he would self-destruct.

"Are you sure you are telling me right?" he asked his friend.

"Would I steer you wrong, man?" Tristan asked. "Besides, I have been with a girl, and you haven't. I'm trying to explain it the best way I know how."

Tristan was right; he had been with a girl, and Vincent hadn't, so what Vincent had to go on—all he had to go on—was indeed Tristan's word. Tomorrow night, he guessed he would see for real what it was like for himself.

"Tristan?" Vincent asked.

"Yeah, man?" Tristan asked.

"What do you think girls would like?" Vincent said.

"Touching a lot, hugging and stuff, kissing, they like that," Tristan said. "Look, man, the happier you make her, the happier she will make you. You already got it made with a woman who will work hard, wait for you, be good to your family. I wish I had a girl like that," Tristan said.

"Thank you so much, Tristan. You have helped me more than you know," Vincent said.

"Get some sleep. Big day tomorrow," Tristan said softly.

The next day was the wedding. It was a busy day! Everybody was running around in circles, not knowing what to do next. Ava was very busy trying to alter a wedding dress to suit Bella. Sophia was busy, keeping away from Tristan as much as possible but also following him with her eyes every step he made. Maria was making the cake with a lovely white center and beautiful white frosting, congratulating the new couple, and even though she and Vincent never had said they were sorry to each other, both of them felt it. They didn't need words or phrases. It was enough to just see each other again.

Gina, who had seemed to turn into a spitfire overnight, was now a little more calm and collected. Now that Vincent was getting married after all, all the things she had fought for and hoped so long for were finally coming true.

Then there was Bella. *God bless the broken road, I guess.* She had waited so long for this, this enchanted day, this wonderful moment in time, and now she was there, she was literally scared to death.

Bella had loved Vincent from afar for what seemed like a thousand years, and she would love him for a million more; the only problem was she had never found out if he loved her. Bella was ready, willing, and able to spend an eternity in her heart with Vincent, married, having his children, based on a life together, never knowing if he loved her in return. That would be such a sad life. Finally, Bella looked down at Ava sewing her dress, making the last few alterations on it.

"Ava?" she said. "I need you to stop a moment."

"Bella." Ava looked up, smiling with pins in her mouth. "I cannot. This dress must be perfect in a little over two hours, and it is nowhere near finished!"

"Ava, please." Bella looked uncertain, scared, frightened, so many things that she didn't want to say but that she knew she had to say. It was almost sickening.

"Bella?" Ava asked. "What is it?"

Bella walked toward the window and peered out at the blazing Italian sun beaming down on the hot vineyards that hadn't moistened at all, only wilted.

The day, which had started off feeling exciting, thrilling, and new, now seemed less impressive, less everything really. The thrilling parts of happiness Bella had once felt seemed just like a whisper of smoke in the air; only she couldn't say it was even the whisper of smoke really.

Bella couldn't even say she was all that was left of two hearts on fire. Bella was one living, breathing, yet loving ghost, and she finally knew it.

"Ava, what drew you to Anthony?" Bella asked softly.

Ava stood up and smiled. "I think it was his dimples in his smile, then finally, his kiss," she remembered.

"Vincent and I have never kissed," Bella said.

"That will change tonight," Ava assured her.

"Ava, please!" Bella cried. "I don't even know if he loves me."

And there it was...all in one phrase, perfectly stated, as if God had spoken those words himself.

"He will grow to love you in time. It will not take long, Bella," Ava said, trying to build her confidence up and help her regain her hope again.

"Ava..." Bella shook her head. "I don't want that, and you shouldn't want that for me."

"Bella!" Ava couldn't believe her ears.

"I want what you have, Ava," Bella said as her eyes glistened. "I want love and to be in love so much and to fall so hard it aches from head to toe! And, yes, I would have loved for that love to be with Vincent, but it's not, and I am foolish to think I could spend the rest of my life trying to make him fall in love with me when he is not. Neither of us deserves that."

Bella softly took off her veil and took down her hair. Then she stepped out of the wedding dress and folded it neatly before putting it back in the hope chest. Bella then put on her own dress and like always, began to sweep. This time, a tear streamed down her face though.

"Bella, please," Ava pleaded.

But Bella tried everything to avoid or ignore her at all costs now. Her mind was made up. There would be no wedding that day, no wedding night that night, no confusion, no regrets.

It was true: Bella did love Vincent with her whole heart and every breath. In every sigh, in every image, in every gaze, she loved him, but she couldn't live with someone who would only "learn to love her," if that were even possible.

"Go home, Ava," Bella said, still never taking her eyes off the broom.

"What should I say?" Ava said softly.

"Tell them...tell them all just what I said," Bella said. "I am in love with a man who doesn't love me back, and I can't live like that. Nobody should live like that."

Bella began to cry more now, desperate tears, and Ava cried with her. Ava covered her mouth and ran out to the house where Vincent, Tristan, and Anthony were all smiles and getting ready.

The door burst open, and Ava's tears began to fall. She tried hard to speak the exact words Bella had said.

"Ava, dear, what has happened?" Vincent asked.

"My love, are you all right? Are you hurt?" Anthony said as he walked toward her.

"It is Bella," she stammered.

"Bella?" Vincent asked. "What's wrong with Bella?"

"Ava!" Vincent shook her. "What is wrong with Bella?"

"Vincent, stop it!" Ava cried. "She knows! She knows!"

Ava turned to Anthony, and she began to cry her heart out. Anthony just held her closely as she wept.

"What are you talking about?" Vincent asked.

"Bella said she couldn't marry a man who didn't love her!" Ava cried.

"What?" Vincent asked.

"She said she loved you with all her heart, Vincent, but she knew you didn't love her, and she didn't deserve that and you didn't either," Ava cried.

All eyes were suddenly on Vincent. Maria stopped icing the cake. Ava turned to Anthony. Sophia stood and just looked at Vincent. Gina let out a small tear from her eye, and then even Tristan began to watch to see what Vincent would do next.

"This is absolutely ridiculous," Vincent said. "I'm going to Bella's."

"She will not let you in," Ava said.

"What do you mean?" Vincent asked. "After we wed, that will be my house as well."

"I am to remind the villagers of this message and this alone," Ava said, looking out at all of the beautiful reminders that there was going to be a wedding there; however, now there wouldn't be.

"Everyone," Ava said painfully, "I have spoken to Bella, and she has given me this message to return to you exactly."

The entire crowd looked directly at Ava, wondering and whispering among themselves as most people did.

The gossip, anything they could think of to say, they were, until Ava yelled out, "Please stop this. Bella has asked me to tell you all something very important."

"Well?" someone in the crowd yelled. "What is the message?"

"Bella said to tell you all she was deeply in love with a man who didn't love her back and that she couldn't live like that, and he shouldn't have to either."

Vincent stood and stared at Ava. Then he looked across at Gina. Gina looked very hurt and distraught. Even if Vincent hadn't loved Bella, Gina sure did, and so she ran to Bella's, immediately after Ava had finished talking.

Vincent had walked into the house, and Tristan had followed him.

"You OK?" Tristan asked.

"I was just left at the altar by my future bride in front of the entire town! Would you be OK, Tristan?" Vincent yelled, as he took off dress clothes and began to put on his work clothes.

"Look, man, you don't have to set in to start work today. You can just take the day off or whatever," Tristan said. "A reset day."

"A reset day?"

"Yeah," Tristan said. "We all need one once in a while."

"Well, just because Bella changed her mind doesn't mean that there is still not work to do," Vincent said in a sarcastic tone.

Tristan did not like this Vincent very much at all.

"Look, man," Tristan said. "She didn't know what else to do."

"She embarrassed me in front of everyone!" Vincent declared.

"Vincent, she was right!" Tristan said.

Vincent gave him a displeased look. "What?"

"That girl loves you so much and works so hard just to please you, and you still can't say you're in love with her! It's only right she call it off before it actually happened. Even though you don't love her, she still says she is in love with you, man, a man who don't love her back, and she can't live like

61

that," Tristan said. "Better to know now than later, ain't it?" he asked Vincent.

"The entire village will now know I wasn't madly in love with her." Vincent rolled his eyes.

"Who the hell cares if the whole village knows, man? She knew it, and that is what mattered," Tristan said. "I told you girls like to be told, 'I love you,' and stuff, 'I want you,' things like that; if you don't do that, they ain't stupid; they figure it out," Tristan said.

"What do I do now then?" Vincent asked.

"Spring break is almost over," Tristan said. "We could go back to school."

That night, Vincent and Tristan left to go back to Julliard. Vincent didn't even say goodbye to Bella; he just left. Tristan, however, had gotten Sophia's address from her, and he began writing to her from New York and talking about her whenever he could.

Since they had gotten back to New York, neither of them had seen nor heard from Paige; however, they both got their old jobs back at the restaurant.

They both sent money to Italy this time. Vincent sent money for the vineyards and so did Tristan. Vincent tried to send money to Bella, but the money always came back "Return to Sender."

The last letter Tristan received, his smile was so wide and happy. Vincent had never seen him look so happy. It had been over six months since Tristan had seen Sophia.

Tristan took the letter and smelled it.

"What on earth are you doing?" Vincent asked.

"I am smelling the letter," Tristan said.

"It's a letter, you idiot," Vincent said. "It smells like paper."

"Sometimes she puts flowers in it." Tristan smiled.

"All this over my sister," Vincent said, shaking his head.

"I am going to marry your sister one day, Vincent, so shut up," Tristan said, opening the letter. A flower fell out.

Dearest Tristan,

I miss you, and I love you. It hasn't been the same since you have been gone. I have wonderful news. With the money you have been sending and the money Vincent is sending, we have saved enough for another vineyard! We have planted the grape vines, and, my love, God has blessed us with *rain*! Anthony isn't having to bring water in anymore, but today our prayers were answered *rain*! The women will try to begin to picking grapes, then emptying them into a large bucket and crushing them with their feet. The wine is fresher that way. It is the old way, but Mama always said it was the best way to do it. Send my love to Vincent, but as always, keep most of it for yourself. I count the days until I see you again.

Love always,

Sophia.

"Rain, man! It rained!" Tristan smiled.
"Yes, and they were able to plant. Why are you so excited?" Vincent asked.
"Vincent, get over it," Tristan said. "You know they needed rain as much as me."
"Oh yes, forgive me," Vincent moaned.

CHAPTER 6

TRISTAN LAY BACK ON HIS BED, AND HE LOOKED OVER AT VINCENT. "So what happens after the vineyards are planted, man?" he asked, seeming so excited.

"Well, Sophia said it rained." Vincent motioned while he sat at the desk. "That means the grapes will not wilt, thank God. Then the women will usually gather the grapes once they are ready to pick, and then they will all pour them into a big tub of a thing and crush them until they have made wine."

"Really?" Tristan closed his eyes. "I could imagine Sophia crushing grapes all day with her feet."

Vincent rolled his eyes. "Sophia is just as flat-footed as me. It wouldn't be any kind of sight to behold."

"Shut up, Vincent." Tristan closed his eyes. "I could watch her do that all day."

"It's crushing grapes, you pervert!" Vincent yelled.

"Big deal," Tristan said. "I ain't imagining nothing wrong."

Vincent was thinking he was anyway,

"They wash their feet before they get inside the giant tub, which then they march around and make the wine. Then they sell it in those containers just like old times. Sometimes the wine is more fresh this way though," Vincent believed. "It might taste a bit sweeter than the ones bought at the store," he assumed, "not nearly as bitter."

"I can't wait to get back there," Tristan said.

"What is it with you?" Vincent asked. "Why are you so obsessed over Sophia?"

"I dunno, man. I just am." Tristan smiled. "It's like I think of her, and nothing else in the world exists. I have never felt like this at all. She makes me believe anything at all is possible, like everything I have ever believed could come true. All she has to do is smile."

"She's not that amazing. Trust me, I lived with her," Vincent added.

"You still upset over Bella, huh?" Tristan asked.

"No, and I will thank you not to talk about Bella," Vincent said, getting up and sitting on the bed.

"Hey, man, thank me all you want, but you are still upset over her, and I know you are," Tristan decided.

"Tristan, you don't know me as well as you may think." Vincent lay back on his pillow and took his hair down.

"Really? I have lived with you and acted with you about three and a half years now. Six more months and I will marry your sister, and I know you almost married a girl you didn't love, because an entire village wanted you to, and you would have if she hadn't stopped you," Tristan decided.

"She embarrassed me is what she did," Vincent declared. "She should get what she deserves."

"How can you say that, Vincent?" Tristan said as he looked over at Vincent.

"Say what?" Vincent asked.

"You act like everybody in that village owes you something, and they don't! All Bella wanted was your love. That's it. She didn't want money or nothing, and you couldn't even give her that! So don't go blaming the rest of us for being happy just because she wanted you to be happy so bad that she couldn't bear the thought of forever and you not loving her," Tristan said most bitterly.

"Say that again," Vincent asked.

"It ain't rocket science. Even I figured it out," Tristan said.

"She worked hard, she took care of your ma, she watched after your sisters, everything you could have wanted. She didn't have a ma or pop herself. She said she would wait for you. You had it made with her man, and you just didn't care at all, and now it's all about you and what she did *to* you, not what she did *for* you, not how much she loved you or was in love with you," Tristan answered. "Even I ain't as selfish as you are, Vincent," he said slowly.

"What?" Vincent said, almost as if he couldn't believe Tristan had said that.

"I may be a jerk sometimes, even an idiot, but I do know what love is, and I do know I love your sister, and she knows it," Tristan said, with as much confidence as he could.

Vincent lay there in the bed, just thinking about what Tristan had said. It really had angered him. Tristan was supposed to be his best friend; however, now he was in love with Sophia and defending Bella, which was something that Vincent was not nearly ready for.

Vincent didn't need Bella's defense. She was an embarrassment to him now, so now when he went back to the village, everybody would know. Everybody would see him and remember the day that Bella had betrayed him and embarrassed him in front of everyone.

He wasn't thinking of all the times she had taken care of Rosa and sat up with her or all the times she had fed Maria or stood up for Ava at her wedding and been there when she and Anthony had lost their baby.

Vincent wasn't thinking of all the times Bella had stood up for him and had sheered sheep for him or how she had learned to shoot for him from Sophia.

Vincent wasn't thinking of all the things he should have thought of or even felt for Bella or how Tristan said there would never be another like her and how he really didn't know how lucky he really was.

Vincent didn't think about Gina's eyes and the hurt in them, about how they had really hurt for Bella and how they had wanted so much to keep their distance from Vincent.

Within the next four months, they were finished with school, and Tristan was even more excited about going back than Vincent! He had heard from Sophia only once more, and he hadn't read that letter out loud to Vincent.

Dearest Tristan,

I love you and miss you more than life itself. We are very busy preparing the wine. Plus the big news is Bella has a new suitor! My love, he is from Sicily. He looks at her a lot like how you look at me and smiles the same way.

Please don't tell Vincent. He would just get angry all over again, and I really don't want that. I want him to be happy for our wedding to give me into your arms, my love. Besides, Bella deserves to be happy. He loves her and has given her a beautiful ring. She is to be married in August, after we are to be man and wife in June. I miss you. Come back safe to me, my love. I love you more than words can ever say.

Love, Sophia

My sweet Sophia,

I love and miss you as well, so much. You are all I think of every minute of every day. I think of you, and I know the best is yet to come! Have no worries, my darling. I did not read your last letter aloud to Vincent; I have no idea how he would have taken that kind of news anyway. Sometimes, I think Vincent has never dared to love anything as much as he has the man he sees in the mirror. Is that a terrible thing to say about my best friend? He blames poor Bella for his embarrassment and shame in the village, and all she did was try to help him by not marrying a man who didn't love her back. Vincent continues to stay mad at me because I see Bella's side. I will see you in about two months. Until then, stay safe. I love you more than anything.

Love always,

Tristan

Tristan had saved a big chunk of his money to buy Sophia a real diamond, and he would have it by the time he went to Teramo with Vincent in about one month.

Tristan had never been so excited, and Vincent just sat fairly silent on the plane ride home, not knowing what Sophia's letter had said. By the time they had gotten there, just like last time, it was about a mile to the village; however, Anthony met them in a car.

"Anthony, you got a car?" Vincent asked.

"I did. I did." Anthony smiled.

"How very modern of you," Vincent said.

"The modern part is teaching all your sisters to drive it!" He laughed.

"They are all learning?" Vincent asked.

"All except Sophia. She wants to wait and let Tristan teach her," Anthony said, looking in the mirror at Tristan.

"That's my girl." Tristan smiled, riding into town.

"How is everyone?" Vincent asked.

"Fine," Anthony said, short and sweet. "Everybody is fine."

Tristan guessed that Anthony didn't want to talk about Bella's wedding either, so quickly changing the subject, Tristan asked again about Sophia.

"Is she still dancing on the grapes?"

"He is such a pervert!" Vincent said.

"If you mean crushing the grapes, yeah, they are all still doing that," Anthony said. "Maria, Ava, Gina, Sophia, Bella, Julia, and Mia and a couple more."

"I prefer to think of it as dancing," Tristan answered.

"You should have heard him in New York. I have never been so tired of hearing about my sister," Vincent said.

"Anything else new?" Tristan asked.

"Oh yeah, you are both going to be uncles again! Ava is due in November." Anthony smiled.

"Congrats, man," Tristan said.

"Yes, Anthony, I am very happy for you as well," Vincent said.

Anthony parked the car, and Tristan jumped out, looking into the grapes for Sophia.

Tristan looked. He saw Maria and Ava. Then he saw the little spitfire Gina, who was sixteen now. Then he looked again and finally heard her.

"Tristan!" She got out and jumped into his arms.

"I missed you so much," she said as she twirled around with grape juice all over her feet.

"I missed you too," he said, and he kissed her right in the middle of the street.

"You must think I am a sight," she said.

"No, I could watch you do that all day, every day, for the rest of my life," Tristan assured her.

"But you're gonna have to let the others do it. I gotcha something." Tristan smiled.

"What is it?" she asked.

"Close your eyes," he said.

Tristan led her to the porch, where he washed the wine off her feet and legs. Then he kissed them, and she smiled and laughed softly as he was making sure all the wine was gone.

"OK, open your eyes." He smiled. "Gimmie your hand."

Tristan was on one knee.

"I love you more than anything in the entire world, Sophia Lorenzo, and I always will. When I am with you, time stops, and it feels like it never starts again. Nobody makes me feel like you do, and nobody ever will. My heart beats a million beats a minute. Every time I see you, I wanna cry. You make me better in every way. I want to marry you. I want you to be the mother of my children. I want to grow old with you, to share all my struggles with you, all my happiness with you. Will you please be my bride?"

"Tristan, you didn't have to buy this." She smiled.

"I know, but you deserve it." He smiled. "Will you marry me?"

"Yes, yes, a thousand times yes!" she cried. "I love you." She smiled.

"I love you more," he said. "Go on now. Get back to dancing in that wine so I can watch."

Tristan watched as Sophia walked over, got into the wine, and showed her ring to the girls in the wine. She was so happy she cried.

"Look, Bella," she said. "It's almost just like yours."

"What? Just like Bella's?" Vincent asked.

Vincent and Tristan walked over to the wine, and Tristan winked at Sophia. Then he saw Bella. She looked different. He knew Vincent thought so to.

Although Bella was "dancing in the grapes," as Tristan called it, she looked very different.

"Hey, Bella," Tristan said, "I almost didn't know you."

Bella looked at Sophia's ring, and it was almost exactly like hers!

"Oh, Sophia!" Bella said as she hugged her tightly. "And hello to you too, Tristan." She smiled. "I do look very different, I am sure."

"You look happy, Bella, and it suits you," Tristan said.

"Thank you." She smiled. "I am."

Vincent didn't stay around long enough to see either ring. He grabbed his bag and walked inside the house. Tristan kissed Sophia again quickly and then followed Vincent. He shut the door.

"If you are finished mooning over my sister and speaking with Bella, have you come to talk to me then?" Vincent said.

"I am finished, for now," Tristan said, a bit on the angry side. "Look, Vincent. You may or may not like it, but I am so in love with Sophia, and every single day just keeps getting better. I am sorry you didn't have that with Bella, but that doesn't mean one day you won't get it."

"Bella has her hair cut short now," Vincent said, enraged.

"So what?" Tristan made a face. "It suits her, right under her ears, a messy bob. Who cares?"

"I never liked it short," Vincent said. "She must have put on at least ten pounds or more since we were here."

"You got a lot of nerve, Vincent," Tristan said, coming over and slamming his suitcase shut.

"What?" Vincent asked.

"You don't want her, but you don't want anybody else to have her, is that it? Is it? She is in love with someone new, and that kills you, don't it?" Tristan asked. "So what if her hair is short now, and she has gained a little weight? Maybe he feeds her. You ever think of that? You didn't even ask his name, which, by the way, was completely rude! Maybe he even tells her he loves her, and maybe that is why she looks so good. Not because her hair is short or her physical appearance, maybe she looks good because she's in love with a man who truly loves her back this time."

Vincent glared at Tristan, hoping to bore a whole right into his soul. Instead, he saw exactly what he didn't want to see, the truth.

"Damn you, Tristan!" Vincent said.

"Fine, my friend. You do that all you want, but before you go damning me all over, remember what I told you. Some girls want money, some want time, some want everything a body can give them, and there are the select few who just want to be loved. Bella is one of those girls, and so is Sophia. I will do whatever is in my power to make her happy," Tristan said.

That night, after Sophia had danced all day in the wine and filled up empty containers, she cooked a meal for just Tristan, and he washed her feet again. The containers were completely filled now, and they were awaiting the wedding ceremony, which would be in June for them and in August for Bella and Rico. Tristan told of all the anger and hate Vincent felt. Sophia just smiled. She knew Bella was happy now. He was too late. There was nothing he could do now.

CHAPTER 7

THAT NIGHT, AFTER EVERYONE IN HIS HOUSE HAD FALLEN ASLEEP, Vincent lay there on his bed, thinking simply about all of the things that Tristan had said.

"You didn't want her, but you don't want anybody else to have her."

Was he really like that? Could it be true Vincent didn't love her, but he was so selfish and self-centered that he couldn't even let anyone else be happy with her either?

Vincent tossed and turned that night until finally he was unable to take it any longer.

He got up and walked down the street, hanging his head down and feeling lower than he ever had in his entire life.

The streetlights were on all around, overlooking the cobblestone road, and thoughts of what might have been danced around in his head.

What if he had kissed her like Tristan kissed Sophia? What if he had held her, turning her around in the middle of the street? What if he had washed Bella's feet and kissed the wine off, not caring what everyone else thought?

Then, he might not have lost the greatest thing that had ever happened to him. Then, he might have been able to be happy, but he knew now that he had lost it. There would never be another person who could make him feel like she did, one who loved him so much, one who was always in his corner, always ready and willing to forgive him when the times got rough.

There would never be someone who loved him as much as she had, so unconditionally, without question, and he had failed to love her the same. Who else would be there now? What if he had formed that same smile on Bella's face that Tristan had on Sophia's?

Tristan had given Sophia every reason to make her love him. What reason had Vincent ever given Bella? He had kissed her hand and asked her to wait for him. In fact, he had only asked her for things. He had never actually shown love toward her or made love to her yet.

As Vincent walked along the street, he looked up into Bella's window and saw the golden light was still on. Even though it was two in the morning, Vincent knew he had to talk to her. He had to know what might have been and in the middle of the night, the early hours of the morning, so nobody saw him. Vincent walked over to Bella's house and knocked softly on the door.

"Bella? Can you please come to the door? I need to talk to you," Vincent said.

There was still no answer, but he knew she was in there.

"Bella, I know you're in there," Vincent had said.

Finally, Bella opened the door and stood in the doorway so that Vincent couldn't come in.

Vincent stared at her. She was a little shorter than he was, darker skinned, the same beautiful black eyes. Her hair was much shorter and almost as dark as his now. It was obvious she had not had to work in the outside nearly as much. He had never noticed before.

"Can I come in?"

"I don't think that is a very good idea, Vincent," she said.

"Please, Bella, I need to speak with you," Vincent asked.

Bella backed away from the door and let him in.

Vincent came into Bella's house and began to look around. Everything looked about the same, except Bella.

Vincent looked around and then back toward Bella.

"What did you want to talk to me about, Vincent?" she asked.

"I wanted to ask you a few questions about myself, to see, to see..."

"To see what?" she asked, somewhat lost in frustration.

Then it hit Vincent, just as if a brick wall had fallen down onto his head, and it was one he couldn't escape or run from or especially not catch. Even with his arms held open wide, the weight of heartache had just buried him.

It felt like the worst feeling he had ever had. Vincent could have sworn right then he was going to die a broken man.

"Bella?" he asked her. "Why didn't you marry me like you had planned?"

"Because, Vincent," Bella answered, "it wasn't right."

"What wasn't right?" Vincent asked as he turned to her.

"Vincent." She smiled. "I loved you with my whole heart, my every breath. All my best intentions were for you and for your family. With every inhale and exhale, I thought of you and your dreams, what they would behold."

Bella walked around and looked outside at the amazing golden moon, hanging low in brilliant black sky.

"Then one day," she said, "our wedding day, I realized I was marrying you for every wrong reason in the book, and I couldn't do that, Vincent."

"What were you going to marry me for then?" Vincent asked softly.

"I was going to marry you for so many reasons." She smiled, "I knew you would be an amazing husband and protector, a wonderful provider and father. Smart and sensitive, compassionate. You had four sisters; you were a wonderful listener. But there was one very important thing, very, very important thing missing."

"What was that?" Vincent asked.

"You cared just a little too much what everybody else thought, Vincent," she said softly.

"Bella—" Vincent began.

"Vincent, stop," Bella said. "I loved you and considered myself blessed to even get to be near you, but, Vincent, you didn't love me. You were going to marry me because I was who the entire village and who your mama thought you should marry, who they thought you would be good with. Vincent, you never even told me you loved me, not once." Bella began to cry.

"We helped each other in so many ways, my dear Bella," Vincent said.

"Vincent, just because we complemented each other doesn't mean we were right for each other," Bella said softly.

"I don't understand. You said you'd wait for me," he said.

Bella turned so as not to face Vincent anymore. She knew what she was about to say was seriously going to hurt, but it was something that she had to say.

"Bella? Bella?" Vincent pleaded. "Look at me again."

"Vincent, I think you should go now," Bella said with a large knot in her throat.

"Bella, please don't do this to me," Vincent asked.

"Vincent," she said, "I did this for our own good. There will come a moment in time when you thank me. You will see, once you find the missing look, the piece to the puzzle, the love you wish to find."

"Bella?" Vincent asked her. "Do you love this man you are going to marry?"

Bella stood still for a very long time.

"Rico is good to me. He looks at me like Anthony looks at Ava. He tells me he loves me every time he sees me." She smiled. "He is not a dreamer. He is a worker on a plantation in Sicily, and he works hard."

"That is not what I asked you, Bella," Vincent said.

"Stop this, Vincent!" Bella yelled.

"So the answer is no then?" Vincent asked. "How far is your hypocrisy willing to go, Bella? You wouldn't marry me because you said I wasn't madly in love with you, and now you will marry this man, but you aren't madly in love with him!"

"That is not fair!" Bella said. "I am still young, Vincent. I deserve babies, a life!"

"What is not fair about it? It's exactly what you said I did," Vincent said.

"It's not!" she answered. "He will continue to be good to me all of my days, and I will him. I can learn to be a good mother and wife."

"I see. You can learn then," Vincent said.

"I can!" she announced. "I will be too busy, being a mother and a cook, quilting, cleaning, crushing grapes when it is time for the vineyard season—"

"What is that supposed to mean?" Vincent asked.

Bella turned away from him. "I won't notice that I am not in love with him is all I mean."

"That is not good enough, Bella," Vincent answered. "At least tell me who it is you do love so that I may know that much."

Bella turned away from Vincent. "You should go."

"I won't," Vincent said. "This man, what will he give you? The finer things in life? What? Who is it you do love?"

"You know I have never asked for anything, type of possessions," she answered.

"Then who, Bella?" Vincent yelled. "At least let me know that."

"It's you, Vincent! It has always been you, and it always will be you, but I can't wait anymore! I can't keep pretending that one day you will come around, Vincent. It's not fair to either of us. I can't keep thinking one day you will love me, Vincent!"

"You said you'd wait for me forever," Vincent said slowly.

"Forever took too long, Vincent," she said, tears streaming down her face.

"So your plan is to marry him then, be a mother to his children, and become a busy homemaker, so busy, you don't notice you don't love him?"

"Vincent, please go," Bella cried.

"Is it also your plan to pretend and wish he is me?" Vincent asked.

"It's none of your business what I do with the rest of my life, Vincent," Bella yelled.

Vincent stared in awe of and total fascination with her.

It really wasn't his business, but it was his life as well, and he watched her slowly, gently moving toward the door.

That night, Bella wore a long white nightgown. It was thin but not enough you could see through it, just enough that it was white. She was in dreadful tears.

"Has he kissed you, Bella?" Vincent asked, almost wanting to pray he hadn't.

"Yes," she answered. "He has, Vincent."

Vincent tried hard not to imagine it, but it was there, in his mind, in his thought process, and he couldn't make it leave.

"Did you kiss him back then?" Vincent asked.

"Yes," Bella admitted.

Bella walked around her small house. "I don't owe you any kind of explanation anymore, Vincent!"

"This was supposed to be my house," Vincent said calmly, "my farm, my sheep, my land, and my wife, my life."

Bella dropped her head and nodded. "I know. Vincent—"

"I was going to work this land, together with you. We would have made a go of it, you and I," Vincent said.

"This is madness, Vincent!" she cried out.

"Why is it then?" Vincent asked her in haste.

"I have a gorgeous man whom I love so much with black hair and the most amazing blue storybook eyes, who loves my farm, and who really, really likes me a lot, but I just can't live like that, Vincent. It is not fair!" Bella cried. "Over and over again, I cry, because I am more in love with you than ever, and at night, I find myself sitting up not having the words, not being able to put the thoughts together in my head of what I could have had, but I don't."

"You are the one who called everything off," Vincent reminded her.

"Yes," Bella said, "because you couldn't even stand to look at me or, worse, even touch me! I thought it best to call the entire wedding off, and then you couldn't even say goodbye. You just left."

"Is that not what you will be doing soon? Leaving with another man?" Vincent yelled.

"It is very different this time," Bella said.

"Why?" Vincent asked. "Why is this time so different from before when I left you?"

"Because he loves me!" Bella said. "You didn't."

Vincent closed his eyes and shook his head softly. "We can argue until the sun comes up, but it won't do us any good."

"You're right; it won't," Bella said.

"The grapes must be crushed again today, so if you don't mind, I need to get in my grape-crushing clothes," Bella said.

Vincent didn't mind. He assumed the grapes would be almost finished. Bella walked into the bedroom and began to put on the clothes. Right when Vincent started to leave, he went back for his hat. Then he saw her, and then it was as if something in him changed.

Vincent looked up. He didn't really mean to see, but maybe this could have turned out to be the best thing for everyone.

It was early morning, and Bella had taken off the gown and thrown it on the bed. As she stood in the early morning sun, she stood bare-breasted with a hint of softness on her and the kiss of the light on her skin. She was more beautiful than he had ever seen her or even imagined her; her porcelain skin with a small beauty mark on her left breast seemed so wonderful and perfect. She was more than Vincent ever imagined.

She hadn't put on the dress she had picked out from the closet yet, and she began to brush her teeth. Vincent watched every-thing about her, knowing he shouldn't but unable to take his eyes off her body. It was incredible. Finally, she slipped the dress over her head and came out of the bedroom to find a dumbfounded Vincent still standing there.

"Vincent? What on earth are you doing here still?" she said. "It doesn't matter. You're here, so as long as you are, could you zip me up?"

"What?" He finally shook his head.

"Come on, Vincent," Bella said. "I have to hurry. Gina will be here soon, and I need my dress zipped."

"Oh yes, of course I can zip it," Vincent said awkwardly.

He slowly zipped Bella's dress, remembering the amazing skin he had seen, now actually wanting to touch her. Then he startled at the knock on the door.

"I'm coming, Gina," Bella answered.

Gina walked in and saw Vincent standing there. Then she gave him a dirty look.

"What are you doing here?" she asked.

"Uh, my hat, I forgot my hat. I was just getting it," he said and then backed into a chair.

"Duh," Gina answered. "Go home. We gotta work."

Vincent walked out, not angry in the least at Gina but amazed by what he had seen of Bella. All these years, he had thought what he wanted was a woman he had never seen before, and he guessed that was true, but something today made him feel a bit differently toward her. Seeing her, if only for a moment, it seemed to bring back things in his mind that he had never even explored, places that now he wanted to go in his head and in his heart and beyond! Tender yet elaborate, mysterious and dramatic, romantic and different. Things were always so simple before, so measured; now they were so unusual and rare.

CHAPTER 8

VINCENT WALKED DOWN THE STREET, JUST THINKING ABOUT what he had seen. He had always thought it so important nothing happen before a wedding, that nothing happen between him and any other woman that would look bad on or for his sisters. He was a terrible example for them.

But to say, "I love you," in any sort of way or to be loved by someone so incredible seemed to be something that was miraculous in so many different ways.

There had been so many nights in New York when he had sat up in bed waving off the feelings of love simply because Bella was not exactly a priority in his life; she was more like a go-to.

Vincent's feelings for Bella were mainly those of just another stepping-stone in life. He knew she worked hard, his mama and sisters loved her, she would be an excellent mother, and in the end, when they died, he knew Bella would be someone he could count on to take care of him.

When the chips were down, Bella was always on his side. Even if she didn't know his thoughts, she wanted to, and she was always willing to listen and finally help him reach a decision. Even if it was the exact wrong one, she listened until she made a way for it to be right.

Had Vincent just now reached this? Were the visions of Bella just now beginning to unfold in his head? How could it have taken so long to see?

Was it only because Sophia and Tristan were together and so happy? Was it simply because Gina couldn't even speak to him anymore without such a harsh tone in her voice, and Vincent really doubted she ever would be able to again? Was it jealousy over a man Vincent had never even met but one who made Bella happier than he ever did or would? Was it the fact that now Vincent knew Bella still loved him, ached for him, and planned on trying to love this man as she still loved Vincent?

Or maybe, possibly, this time, it was the easiest of all. Maybe this time, it all made perfect sense, all because Vincent went back, and for just a quick and simple minute, he either saw what he shouldn't have or maybe what could have helped him all along. All because he went back for his hat!

Bella trusted Vincent even enough to ask him to zip her dress, and she had figured he never would have even dared to think anything else about it.

That was where everything in his mind, heart, and all began to change completely. Vincent's hardened, stubborn heart, which once beat for no other, now seemed to want to race in the wildest of places, not caring if he won or not. It didn't care if it melted, just the idea of the sweetest, most musical love had been Bella, and now, she was gone.

What will become of my withered soul now? Vincent wondered. *I see now Bella loves me, and what if this feeling I am having now is love toward her?* Vincent didn't know, but he swore somehow, that evening, he was going to find out, if it was the last thing he ever did.

After a full day of watching her in the vineyards, Vincent walked into his house. Tristan and Sophia were gone, Gina had wanted to go out, Anthony and Ava were at their house, and Maria was nowhere to be found either.

Vincent walked through to the kitchen and took his hair down. Eating banana bread and drinking milk, he sat still with his thoughts on Bella.

With all his other sisters gone for the evening and Tristan and Anthony nowhere to be found, Vincent thought he may have one more chance to talk to her, one more night to just be around her.

He wouldn't have to tell her what he had seen or how that had made him feel, the reaction he had.

The loud silence went into one ear and traveled completely out of the other, pulling every difficult thought with it! It caused such pain and utter chaos. It was truly maddening and frustrating all at once!

Life had seemed so simple and planned for Vincent at the time of his wedding, and now he was just so lost. Nothing made sense anymore like it was supposed to.

Mama should have still been there. Gina should still have been small and not hating every move he made. Sophia should still be trying to shoot things, not preparing to marry his best friend next month. *I suppose at least Ava and Anthony are getting it right then, being married almost three years in January, and Maria—who even knows about Maria these days?*

Then Maria walked through the door. It was awkward to say the least to see her. Vincent looked up from the table and wrinkled his forehead.

"Hello, Maria," he said gently. He needed to talk to someone.

Maria looked back at Vincent. She was now a beautiful twenty-one-year-old, obviously not the same one he had thrown out over four years earlier.

"I'll just go," she said as she started to turn and leave.

"No, don't go, please. I want you to stay really," Vincent said. "Have you eaten?"

"Not today," she said.

"Come. Sit. I think Sophia made stew tonight, you can have my portion. I really wasn't in the mood for stew," Vincent said as he got up and served her a bowl.

"Thank you, Vincent," she said and began eating.

Vincent watched her closely. She was indeed still beautiful but also malnourished badly. That must mean she wasn't eating enough, getting enough vitamins.

Vincent poured her some milk, and as he was up, she watched every move he made. Maria had never been anyone's fool, but there was a time she had trusted Vincent in every way. That was over now.

"Maria?" Vincent asked. "Where are you staying now?"

Maria looked up at him, almost afraid to answer that question. Truthfully, she wasn't really staying anywhere and hadn't been in the last four years! It was indeed true that she had endured a couple wild nights, but—

"Maria?"

Maria wiped her mouth and put down her spoon for a moment. Vincent watched her like a hawk, wondering what she would do next.

"Vincent," she started, "I don't know if this will make you feel better about me or worse, so I am just going to start and ask you to please don't stop me until I am finished."

Vincent assumed she was about to say she was whoring about all over the village to stay drunk and that was why she looked so thin, but what she did say was completely different.

"Agreed," he said. After all, could he possibly feel any worse than he did right now?

Maria closed her eyes and let out a deep breath, and her words began to flow like some sort of river. The only trouble was it was a river Vincent couldn't get out of.

"Vincent," Maria began, "about five years ago, before you left for school, things were a lot different here. It is true, I had some wild nights, of course, but I never really drank anything. My nights on the town always only consisted of coming in late but never doing anything."

"Maria, you reeked of alcohol." Vincent frowned.

"I reeked of something, dear brother, but it wasn't alcohol," Maria said slowly. "I had been in bars that smelled of smoke and beer, things like that, but I never drank or smoked or anything of the sort."

"But, Maria," Vincent started, "you were out all hours."

"Vincent, yes, I was out all hours," Maria said. "You were at one time my wonderful playmate, who went from being that to trying to be my father all in one night! I loved you as my brother, but as my father, and your house of rules, I didn't.

"Many people say still I got what I deserved, because the famous Vincent Lorenzo made an amazing decision. Those are the same people who have no idea what happened behind the walls of this home or of my heart. Those are the same people who have no idea what they are talking about when they say I was a drunk or a drug addict or how I have slept with half of this village!" she cried.

Vincent was truly shocked and amazed.

"Maria," he said, "I am truly—"

"Sorry?" she said. "It really doesn't matter now, Vincent, OK? It would have mattered when you were not trying to be my father, when the whole town didn't think I had slept with everyone, when I haven't even been with one person, Vincent, not even one!"

"What?" he asked.

"That's right," Maria said proudly and boldly. "I have never slept with one person. I am waiting. When you made me leave, I didn't know where to go! My bag was packed. Our aunts and uncles turned me away as you had. The entire village had made up their mind about me before I could knock on any door, so there was no person to listen to me. Sophia made an attempt to try and tell Mama what was happening the next morning, and Ava would have, but you were always Mama's pick. Sophia had seen me at my weakest, knowing you were not my father. Ava began to ask you if she could go off with Anthony, because she didn't want to be thrown out as well, and I was just too stubborn, too much like you and Papa, I suppose. Mama allowed you to tell us all what to do. I just couldn't deal with it or being the talk of the town anymore! So after you had left to go to America, I went into Sicily, where I met Rico, and then I rented a room from him when I got a job. You came home when you learned Mama was sick, and Bella and Gina and Ava were all there. I had been there but also worked. Bella was to be your love at that time. See, Vincent, things are not always so black and white. Sometimes things are a little off color. I stayed in Rico's house. I rented a room, and I try and help with food, but I am paid very little."

Vincent sat and stared for the longest time, so much had changed, and now he learned he was the cause of Maria leaving. She had not done one thing wrong, although he had.

Vincent remembered back to those times, the sound of his own voice just like it was yesterday. "Go, Maria, and do not come back until you can set a better example."

"Maria?" Vincent started. "I can do nothing about it now, only tell you I feel the lowest of the low. You are right. I was trying to be someone I wasn't. I can't imagine what you have tolerated and how the embarrassment must have been for you. I can only say, 'Please, please forgive me.'"

"What?" Maria asked.

"I am no great Vincent anything! Everything I was supposed to do, it has turned out wrong somehow. My dear sister, please forgive me, and I will try to make it up to you as well as I know how."

"I forgave you a long time ago, Vincent," Maria said as she rushed forth to hug him.

"Now..." Vincent smiled. "It is very obvious you are not being taken care of well enough where you are. You are extremely thin. Sophia will be moved in with Tristan soon, and Ava and Anthony have already moved out. That leaves Gina, you, and me. I would enjoy it very much to work the farm again, and you, me, and Gina all live together."

Maria was elated. She had wanted so much for Vincent to ask her back home for some time. She hoped that he would.

"I would be honored, Vincent." She smiled. "However, Gina and Carlos are together often. It might be that she may have a wedding in the near future."

"Oh dear," Vincent said as he put his arm around Maria. "The burden of four sisters."

"It certainly is a cross to bear, I suppose." Maria shook her head and smiled.

"What will you say when people ask you why you let me move back in the house?" she asked.

"I will say I never should have kicked you out, that it was my fault to begin with and I was a fool to have thought I was like Papa at all and that I need you here with me," Vincent said.

"Vincent, you don't have to do that, really," she said. "The people of this village don't have to know it was your mistake. They look up to you. You have been to America, Vincent! Most of us will never see it; it's enough I get to come back home now," Maria said.

But that wasn't enough for Vincent this time. This time, it had to be better. He had to start owning his mistakes, admitting to his faults, seeking out his flaws, mending his ways; otherwise, the people of this village would always see him as more than he really was.

"Maria?" Vincent called. "I am going out. I don't know when I will be back."

"OK," Maria called back as she was cleaning the pots and pans.

Vincent walked out the door and into the fresh May air. The breeze blew just a little, and the honeysuckle seemed to be late this year. The smell seemed to fill the air like sweet perfume, and it was thick; it must have been because of the spring rain, April showers bringing May flowers. In this case, it was help with the vineyards.

The dew settled on the night grass. The swallowing heaviness that hung all throughout the air was still filled with moisture.

He was walking throughout every crowded moment, every strong and amazing hour, every movement, each step just a little faster than the steps he had made before. This time, he was on his way to go see Bella again.

Vincent had thought maybe if she could realize his faults and his flaws, maybe there would be a chance for them. Maybe if he could only explain his awful ways to her, she may see what he had been this entire time, an honorable man who could finally accept responsibility for his mistakes.

Vincent saw her light was on again, and he went to the door.

"Bella? Bella? Open the door," he said.

"Vincent!" she said as she came to the door. "You have to stop coming over here. People are going to start talking. It is not going to look good for you or me!"

"Bella," Vincent said, "I am sorry. I had to talk to you!"

"Well, come in now, so that people are not hearing us," she said as she looked around.

Vincent began to tell her everything of what Maria had told him, how she had never been with anyone, never drank at all, and how she had only stayed out and away to get away from him. "She was just trying so hard to get away from me and what the townspeople thought of her, so I have asked her to move back in with me. She looks so malnourished and underfed, and I need her as well."

Vincent was overjoyed at the reunion between himself and his sister.

"That is really awesome, Vincent, and I am very glad for you." Bella smiled.

"That is not the only reason why I came here, Bella," Vincent said.

Bella took one look at Vincent, who from out of nowhere had just shown up again that night. His crystal-blue eyes, dark black hair—she truly had no idea why he was there that night. He had been there the night before, and they had gotten angry with each other, but she had no idea why he was there that night.

Vincent did look different somehow, maybe because he had such joyous news? Or rather he was being a little clumsier and more cautious about his words perhaps? It was an odd look for a man of Vincent's standing in the village. Maybe, she figured, in a roundabout way, it was a simplicity of some sort, where boldness had been interrupted.

"I saw you," Vincent admitted slowly, breaking Bella's thoughts.

"What?" Bella asked as she turned to face him, still questioning in her mind what he may or may not be talking about.

"This morning, after we had argued all night, with neither of us getting anywhere, you had gone into your bedroom, and I had started out the door. At first, I did leave, but then I came back when I saw I had forgotten my hat. That's when I saw you. You had taken off your gown and threw it on the bed, and then, I am sorry, but I watched you," Vincent said, this time not looking at her at all.

"I watched you, and even though you hurried along, it was as though time stood very still. I saw the morning light rise over your bare chest. I saw you hurry as you were getting ready, not fully clothed yet. I saw the whole entire thing, and I had to tell you because I felt ashamed not to," Vincent said.

Bella's heart began to beat fast. Her hands began to wring.

"Why didn't you look away, Vincent?" she asked.

"I don't know, Bella," he said. "I wanted to, I tried to, but I couldn't. The image, what little I saw of you, was absolutely perfect."

"I do not understand you at all, Vincent," Bella said in haste. "There is no such thing as perfect!"

"You think I don't know these things?" Vincent asked. "I know them better than anyone at all! This entire village thinks I am perfect, and I am farther from it than anyone here! I told you I saw you, and I apologize."

"Vincent!" she said.

"What?" he yelled.

"I accept your apology," she said.

"Good," Vincent said, as he started to turn the doorknob.

There must be some way to make him stay, some small way to make him stay a little bit longer.

"Do you know that I have never even kissed a girl before?" Vincent said.

"What?" Bella asked.

"I have never before kissed a girl. I was always taught it would be disrespectful. What if it was one of your sisters or mother? I have no idea what to do," he said. "Tristan tried to tell me before you and I were to be married. That conversation did not go well." He smiled, trying not to look embarrassed but failing miserably.

"I can imagine." Bella smiled.

"Yeah," Vincent nodded.

Vincent stared down at Bella. Her smile was still so innocent, and beauty was so complete. There was a whole world inside Bella that now Vincent wished he had known.

"Vincent, come and sit with me. I will show you how to kiss a girl." Bella smiled.

"Bella, you are to be married soon!" Vincent screamed.

"Yes, I am, Vincent. I am only going to kiss you the way a girl wants to be kissed; that's all," Bella said.

Vincent looked at her, not knowing what to do, but he didn't know what to do the other way around either. He supposed kissing her couldn't hurt. That was something he had wanted all of his life anyway. So he hung up his coat and hat and then decided he would indeed listen to what she said and try to learn from her. Kissing her might not be so bad after all if he learned how.

CHAPTER 9

VINCENT AND BELLA SAT ON THE FLOOR FOR A LONG WHILE, NOT knowing how or in what way to begin their lesson.

Bella had been kissed before, but Vincent hadn't, and together, they had never kissed each other.

Bella's small hand lifted up Vincent's magical peach-colored hand. She smiled and held Vincent's hand out in front of her, looking, gazing into Vincent's magical eyes. Bella, in contrast, had eyes as black as midnight, shining with the stars stolen from the sky. Black hair, pink lips, Vincent could swear he had never felt such electricity.

"I am going to kiss you now, Vincent," Bella said.

"OK," Vincent answered.

Bella leaned in and touched Vincent's face. She kissed him ever so softly on the lips and then smiled, biting her lower lip.

"Vincent?" Bella said. "I have never been with a man. I would like to know what to do."

"I suppose there is a first time for everything," Vincent said. "We all have to learn, right?"

"At least we will learn firsthand with people we know, not through gossip," she said.

THE FAMILY

"Agreed," Vincent said.

That night turned into a magical exploration for them both, and it all started with Bella's kiss.

After that, Bella began to take Vincent's shoes off. He watched her. Her hands were already calloused from the plow, but she still took off his shoes and socks. This was one thing that made Vincent smile. A woman who might still have calloused hands from working all day, however, would still rub his feet at night.

Vincent lay close beside her on the floor, trying to remember the words of his wise friend.

"Girls like to be touched and stuff. Go slow the first few times."

Vincent began to kiss Bella a little more, taste her skin, touch her in every way he thought he might bring a sensation, every time making sure to ask her if she was all right, to please promise to tell him if she was hurt.

Bella sighed with great pleasure when Vincent touched her. He asked if he could touch and kiss her breasts, and she agreed. Vincent pulled her on top of him, careful not to hurt her. Then he began to touch her body and kiss her even more.

Bella gasped, holding her head back while Vincent continued touch her, while he watched her movement on top of him. Vincent sat up and held her on top of him. He was falling in love with her so completely, and he had no guilt toward this new man she would be marrying soon anyway. He knew now the love, the subjection, of all the things he and Bella shared. He just needed to be with her one time, just once. Then he would know the way it would be to be with Bella, and she would know what it would be like to be with him.

Bella began to kiss his body, his entire soul, the love of her life, as she rocked herself and tied her legs around him. Then she

95

reached her hands around Vincent and began kissing him more aggressively, wrapping her legs around him.

Vincent thought it was incredible really. Tristan hadn't known at all what he had said, but maybe it was simply because he and Bella knew something Tristan hadn't. Nothing had gone really the way it was supposed to, but that was a long time ago.

Vincent lay back with his hand upon his chest, breathing heavily, but his total and complete satisfaction said it all.

"How would you describe it then?" he asked, still out of breath.

Bella was still sweaty, from the times before, where she had gone, and now she had cheated with Vincent on her boyfriend. She really had no idea what she was to do. Bella did look a tad bit scorned though. What on earth would she do now? She wanted to simply lie awake on her pillow and not feel anything—not a touch, anything. So she rolled away from Vincent.

"Bella?" Vincent asked. "Are you upset with me?"

"No, Vincent, I am upset with me!" she cried, lying there against him.

"I am truly sorry, Bella. Things just didn't seem to work out as I had hoped. I wanted to be inside you, then touch you more, and taste you, all the things I have never done but always wished for!"

"Why didn't you?" she asked.

"If I had tasted you, you might have thought it disturbing. If for only one reason I would have had you a day, I would have kissed you all the rest of my life." Vincent smiled.

"Vincent?" she asked. "Would you lie with me the rest of today? The grapes are crushed. Nobody has to know where you are. You can leave tonight. Then you will not be seen."

Vincent wasn't quite sure what to say, but then those pleading eyes said everything for him.

"Please, Vincent," Bella said.

"Roll over then. I will stay today, and you can sleep in my arms all day," Vincent said.

Bella did roll over and sleep softly in Vincent's arms for the remainder of the day. Nobody really questioned where he was, as it was Saturday. Tristan and Anthony could handle the farm work, and the grape work was almost finished. So as soon as Bella would move about, Vincent would hold her again all day, just like that, and sleep. Bella slept on her side next to Vincent's heart and even though she questioned it, Vincent's very stomach.

Vincent held her in many places as well, her back, her stomach, and what seemed to be her very soul, which was pouring out on his.

Finally, the day was almost done, the moon was slowly beginning to rise over the sand, and it was time for him to go home.

"I must to go now, Bella," Vincent said softly as he kissed her forehead.

"I know, Vincent," she said, looking down. "Thank you for staying with me. I am not so scared of my wedding night now."

"You're welcome, love," Vincent said.

"Vincent," Bella said softly, "it is you I will always love."

"And I love you," Vincent said.

Then Vincent went off into the night, feeling a sense of nothing but sheer pleasure! He had been with an actual woman, and now he thought it best if he told her how he really felt, but she was already spoken for. This would be much harder than it actually looked.

Still, Vincent had to do the best he could to try.

Now it was Vincent who loved another, but that one was to be married to someone else. Now it was he who loved someone and wanted to caress someone who had clearly told him she was going to imagine it was him.

Why would she say that and still plan to marry him? I am here now, and I have changed. I am different. Bella and I made love together. In fact, we invented it! Why would she want someone else now?

"Maria?" Vincent called. "I'm home."

"Good," Maria said. "I have kept things warm for you."

"Thank you," Vincent said.

Maria walked over to the oven and took out a special treat: deer roast with potatoes all around the sides.

"Deer roast?" Vincent said. "What is the occasion?"

"It is for letting me come home. I have soaked it all day to get the wild taste out, and Sophia says she can kill another one soon for here and for her and Tristan."

Vincent nodded. "It looks delicious, Maria."

"It was, but I am afraid now it might be dry," Maria said.

"Why?" Vincent asked.

"Vincent," Maria said, "you haven't been home all last night or today."

Maria was right. Vincent had been with Bella all day and night. He had held her, kissed her, touched her, and tasted her sweet lips that were like wine against his.

"You're right, Maria. I had to spend the night away last night," Vincent said. "I won't do that again unless I let you know where I am going to be." Vincent cut a piece of roast and put it into his mouth. "This really is delicious, no wild taste at all."

Maria sat straight across from him with her hands folded. "You were with Bella, weren't you, Vincent?"

Vincent slowly looked up at her and licked his lips. Then he wiped his mouth.

"What did you say?" he asked.

"Were you?" Maria asked.

"Maria, I don't see where—"

"Vincent, there is no one else here tonight, and whether you like it or not, I know you sometimes a little better than you know your own self." Maria smirked.

"Maria—"

"Vincent?"

"This is absolute madness, Maria!" Vincent yelled, getting up from the table.

"Vincent, I knew there were things about you that had changed when you began to listen to me, when you welcomed me back home. Don't think for one second that I didn't know where you were going. I am sure I still know you like the back of my hand," Maria said.

Vincent put his hand back behind his head. "Yes, I was with Bella."

Maria smiled softly. "I am glad."

"What are you glad for?" Vincent said. "She is to be with someone else, have his children, be his wife, make his quilts, cook and clean for another man. I swear, Maria, for you to know me so well, sometimes it seems you don't know me at all."

"I think tonight we may need to wait up for Gina," Maria said.

"What for?" Vincent asked.

"Gina knows quite a few things she may never tell you, Vincent, but some things she might. She has stayed with Bella through many struggles and obstacles and fought for her when there was no other one to fight for her. She practically lived there when the vineyards dried up, and the heat became so bad. It was something we all just expected," Maria said.

"Gina detests every bone in my body right now, Maria," Vincent said. "Why would talking to her help me with Bella?"

"Because, Vincent, it will make you understand things so much more clearly than what you ever did with Bella. I promise you, there are things Gina knows that you should too."

Because Vincent did trust Maria again, he decided he would wait up for Gina. If nothing else, he could at least tell her what Bella said about being a good wife and mother to this Rico person while wishing it was him.

Vincent wasn't sure, but that may have hurt him the absolute worst. It was like forever now, daily at least, Bella would be waking up, wishing on some other person's star. The night before, when he had kissed her and made love to her, in so many ways, she seemed so gloriously happy. Diamonds in her black eyes to wear; plump, full pink lips; rosy cheeks; sensational hardened nipples; a small mole above her right lip buried beneath the surface of her olive skin—in every way, Vincent noticed every little detail about her—her smile; her neck; her lips, which he ran his fingers across as she said his name, "Vincent"; the way her hands traveled down his torso, and he climbed in and she scratched her nails down his back. Vincent got goose bumps all over again.

CHAPTER 10

"VINCENT," MARIA SAID, "GINA'S HOME."

"Oh hello, Gina," Vincent said. "Maria said you had something you thought I should know."

Gina still looked at Vincent as though she could run through him. Now she looked at Maria that way as well.

"Maria, what did you say?" Gina asked, looking at Maria.

"Gina, I said nothing wrong. I swear it! I only said you knew things, important things, such things that none of the rest of us know," Maria said softly.

"There are some secrets that are meant to be kept, Maria," Gina said.

"And there are some that are meant to be let out, Gina," Maria said.

"Things were different before, you know." Gina shook her head. "I was a kid. I never thought anything bad could happen as long as I was little, but things just kept getting worse!"

Gina looked around solemnly at Vincent. "I think I would have walked through hell for you, Vincent. I really do."

Gina tried hard not to cry, but trying to make a just-turned-sixteen-year-old unemotional is indeed very hard.

"Now, it just is hell," Gina said.

"I don't understand what you mean, Gina," Vincent said. "If I tell you my secret, then will you oblige me and tell me yours?"

"I suppose I can, but I doubt you have anything I care to know," Gina said.

"I was with Bella last night. I had saw her in an intimate way. I knew she was spoken for, and I went to apologize to her. Instead, I did the exact opposite. I stayed with her. And in almost every way possible to me, I thought she was the most amazing thing ever. I do not regret it!" Vincent said.

Gina stood looking at Vincent, and so did Maria. Both of them wanted to say so much, but neither of them said a word.

"Gina." Maria looked over at her baby sister. "You must tell him what you know now."

"Why must I, Maria?" Gina answered. "Because Bella talks to you and you her. Vincent will never know the facts until he hears them from you, and you will never forgive yourself if she marries this man."

Gina knew this time Maria was right. Bella did talk to her. In fact, the two of them traveled with a best friend look on their faces almost every place they went. But there was one thing that Vincent did not know, a large detail in Bella's life, that Gina herself despised and that she also tried hard to protect.

"Are you sure you are ready for this, because once I start, I am not stopping?" Gina said.

"He will listen, Gina," Maria said. "Trust him...Gina, you have to tell him now. He loves her. This must go away."

"When Bella called off your wedding, she was crushed. You were mad, but you didn't love her. She loved you more than anything. She couldn't put you through that. I stayed with her a long time. She got so sick. Then, after about a year, you and Tristan had gone back to school, and here comes this guy from Sicily. Fields look terrible, everything is dry, and he decides one fine day to come up from Sicily. Bella and I were at the market buying what little food we could then, and he decided he would buy us lunch. We both thought that was nice enough and then thought we would go on back home. I was seeing Carlos on and off again. Bella was single again. We all knew she wanted you still.

"Bella started doing things for Rico, smiling at him, things she did for you, things that we would notice but never say anything about. Like she started staying here for his business trips. Bella stopped making apple pie and won't even come to the fair anymore. The thing that is the worst, the absolute worst, is her hair."

"What is wrong with her hair?" Vincent asked, as he was beginning to like it.

"Rico has an awful temper, and the way he takes it out on Bella is usually where no other person can see it. That time, it just so happened to be her hair." Gina looked at Vincent. "Did you think she wanted it that way? Of course not!

"Rico was mad because of something she did, and when she went to sleep, he cut it off! The next day, we went to a different village to have it shaped up, and she has said she liked it."

Vincent looked from Gina to Maria. "He cut her hair?" He stood up.

"Every time she mentions the name *Vincent*, he either pushes her or hits her. Then he comes back and tells her how he is sorry and he loves her and stuff.

"Rico comes back every time and tells her he loves her and that he is sorry, and Bella falls for it every single time. She has attempted to leave before, but he always tells her that nobody would believe her and always buys her stuff. She didn't used to be this way. She didn't used to be so easily fooled all the time. I dread the next two months, because then she is leaving, and I can't go and be with her and the jerk she is marrying. I can't make sure she is alive the next morning. It's not fair that she constantly has to be the one who always settles for the complete asswipe who may say he loves her and buy her a ring, but it is only for show. Her beautiful hair is gone. He gives her flowers only to say, 'I love you,' and 'I am sorry,' and he is rarely ever here. Sometimes he buys her chocolates to say he is sorry as well, but now she shares with me because he calls her fat!"

"No wonder she said she would wish that the man she was marrying was me," Vincent said. "I have never hit her, and I would never."

"Vincent," Gina said emotionally, "nobody ever gives anybody a reason to hit."

"Why would she allow such things?" Vincent asked.

"We tend to accept the love we think we deserve."

"Bella was asleep, and Rico cut her long, thick hair with a pair of scissors," Gina said. "I took her the next day to a place outside of Teramo where nobody knew her. That way, nobody could say anything about her hair. We decided that the story would be it was hot, and that was why she had her hair cut short. I even had mine cut that short so she wouldn't have to go through it alone," Gina said.

Vincent smiled, noticing his little sister's haircut and her amazing loyalty to Bella.

"You truly love Bella?" Vincent asked Gina.

"Enough to stand up with her at her wedding to a man who clearly is violent toward her," Gina remarked.

"Vincent?" Gina asked softly. "Now the question is not how much do I love Bella, but how much do you?"

Gina walked back into her room, and Maria and Vincent were left at the small table.

Vincent seemed to be in shock, not really wanting to believe it. Maria seemed as though she had known the entire time.

"Maria," Vincent asked, "why didn't you just tell me?"

"Vincent," Maria said, "there are some things that Gina knows that only Gina knows. I thought she might know a little more."

"That is nonsense. You wanted her to talk to me again," Vincent answered.

"Maybe I wanted that a little too, but I couldn't tell you all the things Gina knew, especially the end part," Maria said.

Vincent swallowed hard. He had felt those words almost cut through him immediately when Gina said them. "Now the question is not how much I love Bella, but how much do you?"

"Maria," he said, "I cannot go to her again. She is spoken for. I will look like a foolish boy if I go."

"Vincent," Maria said, all the calmer, "if he is being mean to her, shouldn't you know? Before they are married?"

"She never said one word to me about such matters," Vincent said.

"Why would she?" Maria asked in complete amazement. "You are everything to her and a million more things wrapped up into one. She would never tell you, not ever. Shouldn't she tell you, before it does more harm than good?"

Maria was probably right, he thought. *I should go to Bella, ask her about this nonsense I clearly overheard, and she will indeed fix it.*

Gina probably had it in for this Rico fellow ever since Vincent had left, so gossip went around this village like scattered paper.

One piece started at the beginning; the last pieces started like shredded confetti blowing in the wind—all because of one woman loving one man so desperately and so hard, and now he loved her back.

"I am going to Bella's," he told Maria. "I need to straighten all of this out."

"I know." Maria smiled.

Gina just watched him get dressed. "You're going to Bella's?"

"Yes," Vincent said. "And thank you, Gina."

"Just do something," Gina said.

"I will," Vincent said. "I certainly will."

It began to rain heavily while Vincent was walking to Bella's house, trying to come up with words to say to her, like "I'm sorry," and "I love you"—things all left unsaid but that he wanted to say. Then he looked up through the stained-glass window and saw Rico there, dancing to a song with her. Maybe Gina was wrong. Maybe he was only mean part of the time. The other part he seemed to be very normal, and she seemed to be very happy.

A tearful Vincent had lost his chance. Could it actually be true that some people could actually save you? She had saved him. Bella knew him better than he knew himself. Bella had made Vincent feel at peace with the world, safe and protected. She brought out his joy and his laughter. The sides of Vincent he thought were lost or gone forever, they were the ones that showed him the importance of loyalty, hope, and dreams. They made you feel wanted even if every other person in the entire world or town made you feel undesired. All you cared about was that one person. He or she removed what hurt and said your name the way no other soul on earth came close to doing. From the moment he or she walked into a room, that person had brought instant light to it.

He or she did this without any type of effort involved, without even knowing it. That person just became the entire room, the entire event, maybe not to all but definitely to you.

He or she just did something completely and totally naturally. The two souls combined as one.

Bella had shown Vincent love when he had rejected her in so many ways, not even showing her love in return, rather showing her what right he had to be a man. Bella had still stood alongside him.

Now though, things were a little different than before. Vincent wanted Bella everywhere. She was indeed the music to his soul. Vincent imagined her in his mind. If she was beside him, he would never care again.

She was a note he could not stop playing in his head, a song he couldn't stop singing, a touch he couldn't stop feeling, a rhythm in his mind that never ceased.

The rain continued to pour, and Vincent looked up again. Raindrops had settled on his long eyelashes, but Bella wasn't dancing anymore. She was being shoved like a rag doll against the wall and onto the bed.

Vincent ran over to the steps and began to beat on the door, which was locked.

"Bella!" he yelled. "Let me in!"

Rico came to the door in a suit and tie and saw Vincent standing there, soaking wet.

"Can I help you?" he asked, fuming as he opened the door.

But Vincent only saw and considered Bella, shoved and weak, trying to get up.

Her shirt looked like it had been torn in a couple of places, probably from the blows up against the wall. Vincent helped her up, still soaking wet himself.

"What are you doing? She is to be my future wife," Rico said.

"Go, Bella. Put on another shirt, all right? This one is way too damaged now," Vincent said as softly as he could, knowing she was still scared.

"What the hell are you doing?" Rico frowned. "Who are you?"

"Bella, are you ready?" Vincent asked, still wet.

Bella came from out of the bedroom, in another shirt and dress.

"Wait, Bella. You know I don't mean these things," Rico insisted. "Right?"

"I can't keep doing this," she cried tenderly. "Every time, you apologize, and you never mean it. It has to end. We have to end."

"What do you mean?" Rico asked, beginning to get angry again.

Vincent wiped his long wet hair out of the way and stood in protection of Bella.

Bella immediately stood behind him.

"I thought I could raise your children, love you enough that no matter what you decided in our household, I could be strong enough to handle it, but I can't do that anymore," Bella said, taking off her ring. "I could probably always withstand your wickedness to me, but I am sure I would quite possibly die if you were to hit a child, and that would be my fault."

"Bella, get your things. You can stay with us tonight," Vincent said.

Rico reached for Bella, and Vincent caught his fist in the air.

"Listen to me," Vincent said. "She is coming home with me. You are not. From now on, don't talk to her, think of her, or come near her."

"Who are you anyway?" Rico frowned again.

"I'm the man she should have married to begin with," Vincent said as Bella came down the hall.

"So you're Vincent?" Rico smiled.

"In the flesh," Vincent said. "Don't come near her again."

Vincent walked toward Bella and started to take her bag.

"I will come near her anytime I please!" Rico began to grit his teeth.

"I love her, and I am madly in love with her, so stay away!" Vincent yelled, and as he yelled, Rico reached for him.

It was as though every single action happened in slow motion after that. Every. Single. Thing.

There was no sound coming from anywhere, although there was so much to be heard.

Rico had reached for Vincent. Blood was coming out of his mouth and dripping onto the floor. Vincent turned and looked toward the ground and then up again at Bella. There were traces of blood on his shirt, so he took it off and held her. Vincent put Bella's bag on the table. It was filled with clothes. She leaned into his chest and began to cry. Vincent held her and then told her that he loved her, but they must work fast or else someone would think they were the killers, and they really weren't.

Vincent looked outside at the straw and the little house, so beautiful. It had stopped raining for the most part. All that was left was Bella's clothes, a few sheep, and the dead body of her fiancé.

Vincent knew the way it had looked, but he also knew neither he nor Bella would have ever taken a life. Still people trusted Vincent. He had to think of something here. He hadn't heard a thing. Still, Vincent felt Bella was his responsibility right then, so he wrapped Rico in some sheets and then dropped him off a cliff into the Adriatic Sea.

Rico was involved in the Mafia in many ways. This would possibly only look like another hit. Besides, Vincent didn't know what had happened, and he could say that truthfully.

However, that shot that did come from nowhere, and he truly wondered who indeed it was that had shot Rico. He assumed possibly someone who detested him as much as Vincent did. That would have had to have been an awful lot. But he had not seen or heard anything, nothing! It was almost like the clocks had stopped, and the things that had happened, happened in Teramo that night. Vincent had wrapped up a dead body and thrown it over into the sea. Blood had been on a dirt floor, but now it was all soaked up in puddles of confusion and grief.

Vincent ran his fingers through his hair and exhaled. Then he went home to where Bella was with his sisters and Anthony and Tristan. Vincent walked through the door, and he must have startled everyone by his presence, because half the room jumped when he came in.

"Vincent?" Bella got up and ran toward him as he opened his arms to her.

"Yes, my love. I'm fine. Are you all right?" Vincent asked, making sure to look everywhere on her to see if she was OK.

Bella nodded.

"Why don't you go get some rest? I will be in to see about you soon." Vincent kissed her forehead and then said softly, "I love you, sweet Bella."

Tristan sat on the table, and Anthony sat at the table, neither of them really wanting to say anything but both assuming the worst.

Anthony, with his sloppy curls and dark skin, finally broke the silence. "Where is he, Vincent?"

"What?" Vincent asked. "How should I know?"

"Vincent, man, even I don't believe you, and I am your buddy," Tristan said, now wearing Italian farm clothes with his hair pulled back.

110

"Tristan, I am serious. I don't know," Vincent said.

"Take it easy, Vincent," Anthony said.

Vincent walked around the room, not knowing what to do about his family. If they didn't believe him, who would?

Vincent walked around with his hands behind his head. Then he leaned against the table.

"Where are all the other girls?" Vincent asked.

"You sent Bella to bed in your room. Maria and Gina are sleeping in your mama and papa's old room. Ava and Sophia are going to sleep in another room, and that leaves all us out here," Tristan said.

"Are they sleeping?" Vincent said.

"I think so." Tristan shrugged.

"Anthony?" Vincent asked.

"Yeah, I guess so Vincent," Anthony said.

Vincent looked at both of his brothers. He had never had brothers. Now he had to trust them both.

"It's true. I do know where he is now, but I swear on my life I did not kill him, and I don't know who did!" Vincent said.

"Where is he, Vincent?" Anthony asked, looking at the table.

"I dumped him into the sea," Vincent said.

"What?" Tristan asked.

"Would you stop, Tristan? He was already dead. I don't know who killed him," Vincent said.

"Vincent," Anthony said.

"I know this sounds ridiculous, and I did in fact get rid of the body, but I promise you I did not kill him, and I do not know who did!" Vincent felt like he was on trial for something he hadn't even done.

CHAPTER 11

THE ALIBI THE BOYS CAME UP WITH THAT NIGHT WAS INDEED A strong one. Each one of the family had a place in it, perfect timing, perfect everything, perfect loyalty.

Tristan gave each person a place to be in the story.

"Maria," Tristan said the next morning, "you were here cleaning out the deer roast and potatoes, OK?"

Maria nodded. She knew she had cleaned the pots a whole day before, but this was for the family, and she had to do it.

"Ava, you and Anthony came over for supper, OK?" Tristan said. "Since you weren't feeling good enough to cook or anything."

That wasn't true either. Tristan and Anthony had worked in the fields almost all day and cursed Vincent underneath their breath since he wasn't planting with them. But they were going to help him if they could.

"Gina, you brought Bella here. Your close and all right?" Tristan said.

Gina nodded. "Yeah."

That was true. Gina loved Bella more than anything in this world.

"That only leaves my lovely Sophia." Tristan asked, "What do you want to do in this dreaded story, my love?"

"I will do whatever you want, my love." Sophia smiled, wrapping her tender arms around Tristan.

"We will just say you were with me, OK?" Tristan kissed her nose.

Vincent walked into his room to check on Bella. She slept on the side of the bed closest to the wall, and the moonlight seemed to strike a romantic pose on her face.

Her porcelain skin, now darkened a little by the sun, seemed to glow down from the clouds in the amazing velvet sky.

Vincent walked into his room and lifted her up. He let her lay back on his chest. It would be morning soon. They both needed to sleep, but Vincent couldn't. He stroked her hair, and the stars danced all through her face and onto his chest. Vincent kissed her forehead and told her he loved her. Bella fell asleep in the arms of the man she loved finally.

It had finally happened—the end of May—so the beginning of June would be there soon. Sophia was counting down the days. Only fourteen more days. Every day was a day she saw Tristan, and she was very blessed. Tristan was leasing some land from a little farm owner. He already lived there and had a couple of sheep. Sophia would move in when they married.

They already had some goats for goat milk and cows.

Vincent was happy for Tristan and Sophia, and he had already asked Bella if she would marry him as soon as they could get another house built. Vincent worked hard at building a farm for him and Bella. With some of the money he had made in America, he had bought sheep and goats and planted wheat. He traded things like before. Finally, the day in June came, and Vincent was waiting outside the room where Sophia was, just waiting to escort her down the aisle to Tristan.

"Well, what do you think?" she asked, turning around and around in their mother's wedding dress.

"You look very, very beautiful, Sophia," Vincent returned. "Mama and Papa would be very proud."

"Thank you, Vincent." She smiled. "You look beautiful as well."

Vincent smiled and laughed. "I don't know about that."

"You taught me a lot, Vincent," Sophia remarked. "How to be, how not to be, you were there to look up to and always tell me how to do things.

"Remember when I was little and I tried to make biscuits and pie? You still ate some. And then you decided to take me hunting with you. I killed two deer and a rabbit that same week. Remember? You were so puffed up!" Sophia laughed.

"I truly hated the fact my sister could outshoot me." Vincent smiled.

"I couldn't cook and still can't," Sophia said. "I can still out-shoot you, Vincent, in any contest, anything." Sophia smiled.

"We do not know about that anymore." Vincent pointed at her.

Sophia looked through the window, and she stared at Tristan. His hair had grown out a little. It was a dirty blond. He was tan from the sun and had dimples on each side, with beautiful, mystical gray eyes, and he awaited her at the end of an altar.

"Vincent," she said softly, "you see that man who waits for me." Sophia nodded her head toward Tristan.

Vincent looked down that way.

"I love him with all of my heart, and I will spend the rest of my life trying so hard to make him the happiest man alive. When you give me away today, I will become one with him, his bride, his wife, the mother of his children, his everything. My entire future rests in his eyes, but, Vincent, I do have a confession to make."

Vincent looked down at Sophia. "What is it, Sophia?"

"Before I walk into Tristan's arms, I gotta tell you. The night you had gone to Bella's, and Rico put his hands on you, it is my fault. I killed him. I put my silencer on my gun, and just like a deer, I shot," Sophia said.

"You what?" Vincent asked.

"I need you to promise you will never tell Tristan," Sophia said. "I want to be what he wants me to be."

"Sophia! How could you do that?" Vincent asked.

"Do what, Vincent? Protect the man I grew up with, or protect the man I am going to have a future with? Because in both ways, this little sister of yours does not miss when she aims her gun," Sophia said.

"Sophia!" Vincent said, looking quite astonished.

"I don't know anyone else in this entire world who would kill for me, and you did. Thank you, my dear sister," Vincent said.

"Remember, Vincent, today, when you give me away, he never knows, and after today, he is the man I would kill for, but before, it was always you. Are you ready to give me away?" She smiled.

"Nowhere near it now," Vincent said.

Vincent began to walk Sophia up into Tristan's arms, and although he hadn't thought of it, he certainly should have.

Sophia is a good shot, almost as good as me, she knew everything about a gun, and she also hid it very well. Sophia, you were the one who risked your life to save mine?

Sophia loved Tristan with everything she had in her, but there was a time she had loved her family a little more, enough to take a life for Vincent. No other person had ever done that. Of all Vincent's sisters, he assumed he had the least common bond with Sophia.

Maria was just a couple years younger, Ava barely a couple years younger than her, and then Sophia. He remembered her being around a lot and often trying to make her feel better by taking her hunting or eating her terrible cooking.

He remembered teaching her how to clean a deer and a rabbit. But he never thought she would learn how to put a silencer on and kill for him; however, she did, and she was right: she hadn't missed; the bullet had stayed right inside his head.

"Don't tell Tristan," she had said. "After today, that is the man I would kill for."

"You may kiss your bride, Tristan," the priest said.

And Tristan looked like the happiest man who ever lived, raising Sophia's veil and then kissing her.

Everyone began to applaud and smile.

Later on in the evening, Tristan walked over to Vincent and shook his hand. "I guess we're brothers."

"There really is no other person I would rather have as my brother," Vincent said.

"Me either," Tristan agreed.

"We had fun in school, but now it's time to settle down, right?" Tristan asked.

"Yes," Vincent said, "settle down."

"You OK, man?" Tristan said.

Vincent was indeed fine. In his mind was just a loyalty that the wrong sister had for him, and now he couldn't tell anyone.

"Tristan?" Vincent said as Tristan started to walk off.

"Yeah." Tristan turned.

"Be careful tonight. She is still my sister," Vincent said.

"I know," Tristan said. "I'll be careful."

After the cake and lovely June day, Vincent couldn't help but think of what Sophia had told him. It was all so secretive and so loyal at the same time.

Sophia wouldn't stand for the one man in her life to be mistreated, so she had killed him, took a human life. But she had also told Vincent that she would never do that again; if she ever, ever killed again, it would be over Tristan now, and Vincent understood.

Her life had been all about him before, and now there was someone new to take his place. The way it should be. Vincent had misjudged Sophia so many times, never knowing that this could possibly be whom he had taken for granted in the end. He wondered now if she would kill again for Tristan or her children; he didn't think so. But Vincent would not put anything past her now. Her love for Tristan was above all else.

"Vincent?" a sweet voice said from behind.

"Hello, Bella," he said as he put his arm around her.

"It is indeed a lovely wedding, isn't it?" She smiled.

"Yes, it is beautiful," Vincent said.

Bella looked deep into Vincent's blue eyes. "A beautiful sea."

"What is?" he asked.

"Your eyes, of course." She smiled. "A beautiful sea, they make me want to drown just looking at them."

"Go ahead, and jump in. I will save you," Vincent said, leaning his head down onto hers. "I love you, Bella."

"I love you, Vincent," Bella said.

"I want to go back to our place." Vincent smiled.

"Vincent!" Bella said, biting her lip and laughing. "We can't. It's Sophia and Tristan's day!"

Vincent smiled. "Please, Bella, it's all fixed now, and no one will ever even notice we are gone."

Bella smiled and leaned in on Vincent's shoulder. Then he whispered softly into her ear, "I want to be with you again, Isabella."

Bella looked up and immediately could have crashed into waves Vincent knew as eyes. That was all it took.

Not only had he said he wanted to be with her again, but he had also called her by her name, a name her father and mother had called her, and when he did, she truly thought she would melt.

"You called me Isabella?" she said.

"I did," Vincent admitted. "Was there a problem with it?"

"No." She sighed. "It sounded the most beautiful when you said it."

Vincent smiled, and then he said, "Shall we go then, Isabella?"

"Yes," she said.

Vincent was right; they would never be missed.

Ava had gotten tired, so Anthony had taken her home. Gina and Carlos had gone out riding a bicycle. Maria was helping to do cleanup with the other women of the town, all indeed saying how beautiful it truly was. Sophia and Tristan had finally danced underneath the lights and were now gone into their little home.

Vincent and Bella had hurried off to her home, which probably next month would be theirs.

Vincent and Bella walked into the house, and she looked up at him and took off her panties. He unzipped his pants, and they began to kiss each other intensely and madly. Vincent began to touch her as she stood, arms up against the wall.

Bella began to sigh and close her eyes, which only led to Vincent believing he must be doing something right. He took off his suit and went under Bella's dress.

Bella had never felt so amazing, so much pleasure! The first time they were together was indeed incredible, but this time was so much more, so much more of the things one might have never known.

Vincent came out from under her dress and kissed her mouth. Then he picked her up and carried her to the bed.

"We will need to get this dress off now." He smiled, and so did she, and they began to take it off.

Vincent began to kiss her neck and breasts, and as he did, Bella smelled her scent on him. It was a place no other man had ever been or ever would be again, only Vincent.

"I could look at you for hours, Isabella, and never tire of it," Vincent softly said.

Bella ran her hands all over Vincent's shapely body. His hair was down now. His pink, full lips; his rosy cheeks; his muscles; his almost peach skin; and those amazing blue eyes—she was in total awe of him.

Isabella looked away, tears falling onto her pillow.

"My darling, are you crying?" Vincent asked as he climbed off her and touched her chin. "You are! Isabella, have I hurt you? Whatever is wrong?"

"No, Vincent." She smiled, as she rubbed his face gently. "You didn't hurt me at all."

"But you are crying though. I see you," Vincent said, looking at her.

"Yes." She nodded.

"Please talk to me and tell me why," Vincent said.

"Vincent," she said, "I love you so much, and I never thought it could be this way."

"What way?"

"I never thought you would ever love me the same. I never thought you could ever want me. I never thought I would get to have a heaven on earth until you. And now, the way you have made me feel tonight, the amazing pleasure of it all, the sighs, I don't know that I can ever live without that again. I feel as though God has made you just for me," she cried.

"I want to be with you in my darkest times, in my best times, and in every time, because to me, you are perfection, and I want to die with you at the exact same moment, so that I may hurry to the other side and fall in love with you all over again.

"I am not crying because you have hurt me, my love; I am crying because I do not think I could ever, ever live without you again," she cried.

Not even Vincent could keep from crying after those words. He kissed Bella like he never had before. Then he climbed back on top of her, and through his own tears, and hers, she welcomed him inside her.

"I will always love you, Isabella, and I will find you throughout eternity and fall in love with you instantly all over again." Vincent smiled, climbing deeper inside her.

"I will always love you, Vincent," she managed to say through tears. "Always."

The sexual position Vincent was in was now the most unique of all. It was called the swivel and grind, and when done correctly, there was simply nothing in this world that felt better—a missionary position that goes in deeper and deeper and touches you more and more until you are finally unable to move anymore. Your legs become numb.

Everything in them was gasping for air. This was something Vincent wanted as well.

Vincent finally helped her by pushing her legs up, seeing her weakness, and she could still smell her scent on him as she pulled his hair and kissed his neck.

Vincent was in fact her weakness completely, and he always had been. Isabella was becoming his too. She sighed again and wrapped her legs around Vincent, and he smiled, sweat pouring off him as he kissed her.

"You must like that?" he said.

"Yes, I do," she said. "In fact, I crave it now."

"Well, I will try and make sure I can always make that happen," Vincent decided as he kissed her one more time.

"Isabella?" Vincent asked. "I don't want to wait until July to marry. Our farm and house is finished. Can't we marry by the end of this month?"

"Vincent, are you sure?" she said.

"Yes, my love. I don't want to spend another day without you by my side, in my arms, in my bed, as my wife." Vincent smiled.

"Today is the tenth. Why don't we marry on the twentieth?" She smiled, lying in his arms.

"The twentieth it is then." Vincent smiled. "We shall announce it tomorrow," he said, kissing her hand.

"OK." She smiled. "I love you so much."

"I love you."

The next morning, Tristan was up bright and early, shoveling the hay for the cows and sheep to eat, while Sophia was gathering eggs and feeding the chickens. They smiled at each other a lot, and Sophia even laughed a little, remembering the night before and caught a kiss from Tristan as he was brushing the cow.

"I'm going to make breakfast," she said.

"Good," he said. "I'm starving."

"Good morning, Brother," Vincent said as he walked up to Tristan, milking his cow.

Tristan looked over the cow, and he saw Vincent's smile was unusually big that day.

"Good morning," Tristan said. "You are looking very happy today, brother."

Vincent tried to wipe the smile a little from his face, but it wasn't possible; he was so happy. He was ultimately glowing. He put his head down. He looked behind him. He even shook his head, but that smile would not fade.

"Vincent?" Tristan smiled as he got up and walked toward the gate. "What are you not telling me?"

"Nothing!" Vincent laughed. "So were you gentle with her as I said?"

"You definitely don't have to worry about that one," Tristan said, pointing toward Sophia.

"Something is different. Tell me," Tristan said. "Oh man, I know what it is!" He laughed. "You got laid!"

"Tristan, stop it!" Vincent said but then began to laugh.

"Am I wrong?" Tristan asked.

"No, in fact, but I wouldn't put it that way. We made love. We invented it," Vincent said.

"You are crazy, man." Tristan smiled. "On my wedding day!"

"Shut up, Tristan! Besides it's nothing like you said," Vincent said.

"What?" Tristan said.

"It is so much better! That is why we are moving the wedding up to the twentieth of June instead of July."

Tristan continued to laugh. "Congrats, man. I will help you any way possible."

"The house is finished, and we have a few sheep. Deer season is coming. The wine will sell again next year for a good price, and so will the wheat. Between the three of us—you, Anthony, and I— we should be able to see a profit by the end of this year."

"Just tell me, it is Bella, right?" Tristan smiled.

"Of course it's Bella!" Vincent said. "And it is the best meal I have ever had."

"Damn you, Vincent," Tristan said. "I knew you had it in you...I ain't gonna say nothing, man, except I am so proud for you guys."

"Brothers don't go kiss and tell, you know," Vincent said.

Vincent turned around and began to walk back toward the road, putting his hands in his pockets. He couldn't help but smile. Bella, Isabella to him, was a daydream, a wonderful nighttime fantasy he so hoped was real, that he didn't have to wake up from. She was the type of reality that you had read, but you never wanted to reach the end. *My Bella. What if everything beautiful was fiction and the reality was just all pretend? Oh my amazing Bella.* Vincent seemed to hurry a little faster. He had to make sure she was there, that what was happening to him was really happening and it wasn't pages in a worn romantic novel filled with fictional characters that weren't really there.

Vincent ran quickly into the house and saw Bella mending a sock that had a hole in the toe, and he smiled, looking at her angelic face. "You are in a very big hurry, my love."

"I just had to make sure you were real and that you were not a dream after all," Vincent said.

CHAPTER 12

BELLA SMILED HER BEST SMILE AT HIM.

"As long as you want me, I am yours for the taking."

"I will want you forever then." Vincent smiled.

"Do you promise?" she asked.

"I promise," he said. "But right now, I am starving. Would you please make breakfast?"

"It's in the stove keeping warm, silly." She smiled. "I already made it."

"Thank you, love." Vincent kissed her head.

It was eggs, bacon, and biscuits.

"It looks delicious. Where did you get the bacon?" Vincent asked.

"The vineyards did so well this year, my love, that I bought a hog. Gina and I divided the meat. That is some of the pork from my half."

"I must love the smartest woman alive." Vincent smiled.

Carlos burst into Bella's home, almost totally out of breath and covered in blood.

"Carlos, you don't burst in someone's home like that," Vincent said.

"Bella! It's Gina! You gotta come."

Bella immediately stood up.

"What about Gina?" Bella asked, following Carlos with Vincent not far behind.

"Carlos!" Vincent yelled. "What is wrong with Gina?"

"Let me go, Vincent!" Carlos yelled. "I am just as worried about her as you, probably more."

"How is that even possible? I am her brother," Vincent said.

"You may have had her little girl days, but she is to be my wife and have my children. I don't know what I would do without her."

Carlos ran through the door.

"He's right, Vincent," Bella said. "What if it were me?"

Vincent loved Gina, but he couldn't even imagine the thought of life without his Bella now, so he allowed Carlos in and stood in the kitchen. He saw Tristan and then Sophia come in.

"What happened?" Tristan said. "Is she all right?"

"We don't know," Anthony said. "She was only waiting for Bella and Carlos, then Sophia and Ava and Maria."

"Tristan?" Sophia asked.

"Go," he said. "I will be right here waiting for you."

All three men were pacing in the kitchen. There was no sound coming from the bedroom at all, almost like no breathing at all, which was incredibly odd. Gina was small, but her mouth was so capable of many things.

Finally, Maria, Ava, and Sophia came out of the bedroom and looked up at Vincent, Tristan, and Anthony.

"She's asking for all of you now," Maria said softly.

"What?" Tristan said in disbelief.

"Come on." Vincent grabbed his arm, and they all walked into the room where Gina lay.

"Bella? What happened?" Vincent asked, knowing he could get the truth from her.

Bella sat there, holding on to Gina's hand. Bella began to cry just looking at Gina. She was losing color fast, and her once very tan self was barely able to open her eyes now.

"Carlos?" Vincent asked, looking from Gina as she lay on the bed to him. "What happened?"

"Anthony?" Gina called.

"Yes," Anthony said, going toward Gina. She was covered in blood and scratches.

"I have to tell you something," she managed to say.

"OK, Gina, what is it?" Anthony asked.

"I'm sorry," she said.

"What for?" Anthony asked.

"I wrecked your car," she said, looking over at Anthony.

"It's OK, Gina. I promise," Anthony said.

"I didn't mean to, and I don't even remember what happened," she said.

Carlos looked at Gina almost like his future was being taken from him.

"It's OK. You rest now, Gina," Anthony said. "I forgive you."

Gina blinked a couple more times. One eye was swollen shut, but the other was open, and then she saw Tristan.

"Tristan?" Gina said.

"Yeah?" he asked, going toward her, not knowing what else to say.

"I have always hated you and everything about you," she said as she began to speak more slowly. "But you have always been the one thing that could make Sophia the happiest, and you came and sent money, and you made this your home, so I have always admired and respected you."

"Thank you, Gina." Tristan smiled with a small tear rolling down his cheek as he sat beside her. Then he got up and cleared his throat.

"Is Vincent here?" Gina asked.

"I am here, Gee Gee," Vincent said, as he walked toward her bed and sat beside it.

"Gee Gee." Gina tried to smile. "You haven't called me that in a long time."

"You're not very little anymore," Vincent said.

"I wrecked the car," she said.

"It's replaceable; you're not," Vincent said.

"Vincent," she said slowly, "I know you love Bella and always will."

"Yes, I do," Vincent said.

"I love you, Big Brother. I always have, no matter what I said, and I always will," Gina said.

That meant the world and everything in it to Vincent. He was sure Gina hated him.

"I love you, Gina," he said. "Gina? Gee Gee? Tristan, get the doctor."

Tristan ran out.

It seemed like it didn't take any time for the doctor to be back, and then he began to ask everyone to clear out.

"I can't leave her," Carlos stated.

Vincent and Bella went into the kitchen with the others. They had fallen silent. Every sister stood beside her husband, except Maria, who was just thankful to be in the house again.

Ava stood beside Anthony, who sat at the table with his mouth to his hand, clearly praying she would be all right. Sophia stood crying at the sink while Tristan stroked her hair and then held her as she cried. Maria tried to seem busy while making lunch for everyone, but in the end, she kept dropping things.

Vincent watched Bella as she bit her nails and spit them across the room, a nasty habit she had always had from the time he had first met her still to this very day. In fact, Gina now did it too.

Vincent walked up behind her and took her nails down. "You are going to bite them in the quick, my love," he said.

Bella smiled a faint smile and put her hand down.

No sooner than she had, the doctor came out of the room in which Gina lay.

"Well?" Bella said hopefully.

"I am sorry," he said. "She has lost too much oxygen to her brain."

"No!" Bella pushed Vincent off her. "Gina! Gina! Come back to me please!" Bella began to scream. "Gina, there is so much more we haven't done. Please, Gina, please wake up. Don't leave me, Gina," Bella cried.

Tristan and Anthony started dragging her out. Ava and Sophia cried the most over Bella's reaction. Bella had lost so many people in this world, and now she was losing Gina as well—her best friend.

Carlos walked out of the room where the doctor had stood listening to the screams of Bella. He looked to be in total shock.

"Carlos," Vincent asked, "what happened?"

"I don't rightly know, Vincent," Carlos answered. "She was so happy. I had never seen her smile as bright. I was letting her drive today, and she was having so much fun."

"You let her drive," Vincent said. "She would still be alive if not for you."

"Vincent," Dr. Sims said, "turn him lose! Gina suffered from the same disease your grandmother had. She just had it later in life."

"What disease?" Maria said.

"None of us really know what to call it. Some call it fits. Some call it the falling sickness, and for some, they call it a seizure. Gina never should have been driving that car or any car anyway. If she hadn't wrecked herself, she may have wrecked with someone else and killed them. It's possible she may not have lived with herself knowing she killed someone else."

"Is there a medicine?" Sophia asked.

"Not yet," he said slowly. "We only know what it is called so far. We have no way to treat it. As you see in Gina's case, she lost oxygen to her brain and a lot of blood in the car crash."

"If our grandmother had it, then why is it none of us have it?" Ava said.

"I don't know that you don't," Dr. Sims said. "But I don't know that you do either."

"It took Gina's case sixteen years to show up. None of yours may ever."

"Again, I am very sorry," Dr. Sims said as he walked out of the house.

"Please, let me go! Please let me go!" Bella cried as Tristan and Anthony held her and took medicine from Dr. Sims to give her later, a sleeping powder.

Bella's dress was ripped, and she was crying tears that only a best friend could.

"Let her go, boys," Vincent said, holding out his arms. "Come to me, Isabella."

"Vincent? Please let me go see Gina," she said as she began to look for a way past him.

"Bella, Gina's gone," Vincent said in a gentle tone. "It's just all of us now."

Bella closed her eyes and shook her head no.

"Vincent," she said a little more calmly, "don't lie to me."

"Sweet Bella, I swear I'm not," he said.

"Gina was always there. No matter who left me, she never did. Gina loved me. When the entire rest of the world turned from me, made a fool of me, Gina didn't. So all of you take it back. She is not dead. She never left me. Take it back. You are all lying to me. She is not dead; she will be back soon. I know it. I know she will." Bella looked through the faces at the men she would soon call brothers, the women she would soon call sisters—and then at Vincent.

Every single one held sorrow and pain for her, a true hurt. Bella actually believed she was being lied to, not by one but by all of them.

Vincent started toward her. "My love, I am coming toward you now."

"Anthony," Tristan said, "go put this in some tea."

Anthony ran up the steps and fixed Bella some hot tea. Then he poured the sleeping powder in and gave it to Tristan, and he took it to Vincent. Vincent told Bella it was tea but didn't tell her what was in it. He was afraid she might not drink it.

As soon as she did, she collapsed into Vincent and Tristan's arms, and they took her back to the small farm.

"How long do you think she will be out like that?" Tristan said.

"I don't know," Vincent said. "I know I will be out here when she wakes up though."

"Are you not going to help plan Gina's funeral?" Tristan asked.

"Tristan, you and Anthony will be there to help the girls plan, and I will be there in two days to be a pallbearer. Just make sure Carlos is one as well," Vincent said.

"Bella will want to go," Tristan said.

"After today," Vincent said to his friend, "I am not even sure she will be able to go. Tell the girls where I will be. I know they will understand."

True to his word, Vincent sat up all night in the same rocker that Bella had been mending his socks in. He did not want to bother her so she could get as much sleep as possible.

It had come as a blow to all of them about Gina, none so hard as Bella though. The day had started off so perfect and then had ended with so much misery and grief. Pain and total loss. Complete despair to such a bitter day.

Vincent remembered back to when Gina was first born and how he had prayed for her to be a boy. Needless to say, she wasn't; she was a beautiful little brown-eyed girl who followed him around everywhere. Sometimes it got somewhat annoying, but other times, he had to admit, he loved it.

Vincent was relieved to hear today that she loved him. He also hated thinking she had hated him. Gina was a spitfire in this world, and he would miss her greatly. In a couple of days, he, Tristan, Anthony, Carlos, and a couple more of Gina's friends would be taking her to the grave by Mama and Papa's.

Vincent walked into the bedroom and looked at Bella. She was so sweet and so innocent now, not tempting at all. She was sleeping and heartbroken. Even in her sleep, you could still see the pain of her missing Gina.

My baby sister had been Bella's sun in the snow. Gina had been Bella's home when I was gone, the road whenever Bella needed a place to go to, and a sanctuary when she needed a place to hide.

When I let Bella go before, it was Gina who showed me the way back to her, and I will be forever in her debt. Bella had been a lamp to my feet. Gina had said somethings that did in fact hurt but needed to be said.

Today would be the day of the funeral. Carlos's sister Anna was planning on staying with Bella and giving her more sleeping powder if she woke up, while Vincent was carrying Gina from the church to the graveside.

From what Vincent had gathered, the girls had put together a beautiful service, a lot like Mama's. Carlos didn't say much, but they let him walk first in line to carry Gina, and then as they all stood there, they lowered her into the ground right beside Mama and Papa. Tristan, Carlos, Anthony, Vincent, Angelo, and Mark were all there for Gina.

After the service, Vincent decided he would hurry home to check on Bella and see if she was all right.

He walked in. Anna still sat quietly in the rocker and said, "She hasn't made a sound."

"Thank you, Anna," Vincent said. "You may go now. I can take it from here."

"You know, Vincent," Anna said. "I have always had a certain crush on you."

"I am flattered." Vincent frowned. "But this is to be my home, Anna, mine and Bella's together."

"She is so sound asleep she wouldn't hear anything," Anna said. She wasn't nearly as beautiful as Bella, and Vincent didn't love Anna.

"Anna," Vincent said as he backed up, "maybe you didn't hear me. I love Isabella with all my heart. I would never do anything to hurt her."

"Isabella now, is it?" Anna said. "She will never hear us. I will not tell."

"Please get out!" Vincent said, trying hard to make her leave.

Then Bella came from out of the bedroom, cleaning a sharpened knife.

"Who are you?" Bella asked, still in her nightgown.

"I am Anna. I was just staying with you a little bit until Vincent got back," Anna said.

"Oh yeah?" Bella smiled.

"Yes," Anna said.

"Guess what," Bella said.

"What?" Anna asked.

"He's back now." Bella smiled.

"Oh, so he is." Anna laughed.

"Oh and, Anna," Bella said.

"Yes?" she asked.

"The next time you try and come near Vincent..." Bella smiled. "I won't be so freaking nice."

"What?" Anna said.

"Don't play dumb. I heard it all. He's taken, get it?" Bella said.

"I got it." Anna frowned.

"Good," Bella said.

"Well now, who is sticking up for who?" Vincent asked Bella. "And what was the knife all about, Isabella?"

"What can I say? I got a man that makes me wanna kill," Bella said as she kissed Vincent.

They talked later about the way the funeral had gone, that it was truly nice for what it was.

Bella understood why Vincent hadn't taken her to the funeral; it probably would have been awful anyway.

They did marry on June 20 of that year, but Isabella would not have it any other way than to be standing in the church with Gina's picture beside her, just as planned, as her maid of honor.

Isabella married Vincent with Tristan Hart as his best man.

In August, the wheat brought in a nice little profit, just like Vincent had predicted. They sold it and still made a little money for winter crops, cabbage, and so on. In September, both Bella and Sophia found out they would be mothers in the Spring, and Anthony and Ava had a beautiful baby girl November 2, which nothing do Anthony but her name be Gina. After such a cold winter, in the spring Sophia had a baby boy in March named Christian, and three weeks later Bella had a beautiful baby girl with Vincent's amazing eyes. Vincent decided they should name her Rosa, meaning a beautiful flower after his precious mother. In May, Maria married Angelo Vargus. So much can happen in a years time.

It still makes Bella melt only when Vincent calls her Isabella, and she still has a jealous bone when it comes to him, but he doesn't mind too much. In fact, he loves it and loves her. Once a week, they all get together, have a nice meal together, and explain their weeks to each other, which is usually not hard since they work together.

The conversation usually goes something like this. They were all at Tristan and Sophia's.

Everybody was talking over everybody, but they in turn knew what everybody else had said.

"Mmmm, is that a deer roast I smell?" Vincent asked Maria as she was bringing one in.

"Yes, it is. I cooked it," Maria said. "Sophia killed it."

"My baby can outshoot us all," Tristan said.

"That's for sure," Anthony said. "Look who is walking all her own, no hands."

"Good job, Gina," Tristan said.

"Do I smell Bella's potatoes?" Angelo said.

"Yes, in fact." Bella smiled.

"Vincent, could you please watch Rosa for a minute?" Bella asked.

"Come see Daddy, Rosa." Vincent lifted her up.

"What should we do this year about the wheat prices if they go down? All of us will suffer," Tristan said bluntly.

"What if we planted potatoes?" Angelo said.

"Oh no," the men moaned. "Not potatoes, they would be way too much back-breaking work."

"We have a plow and seed for corn," Anthony said.

"What will we do if we go through another dry spell?" Ava asked.

"We got through it before. We could again, and there are twice as many now as there once was," Bella said.

"What does the almanac say this year about rain?" Sophia asked.

"I don't know, but if there are more of us working, then there are more to watch the babies, I think," Maria said.

"Tristan will know what the almanac says about rain. Where is the book, babe?" Sophia asked.

Tristan got up and was looking at the almanac for that year. "It says we are expected to have a good rainy season this year, better than last year."

"See, better than last year," Sophia said.

"That is not always right, Sophia," Anthony said.

"Hey, don't correct my wife at my table." Tristan frowned. "It ain't always right though, baby," he whispered.

"But you are, my love." Sophia smiled.

"See? My wife has faith in me," Tristan said.

Bella looked at Vincent and smiled.

"Ava tell them the book is wrong sometimes. Remember the awful drought about three years ago? We had to bring in water," Anthony said.

"You are right, Anthony," Ava agreed.

"Is there nothing we can agree on?" Vincent asked.

"The food is awesome," Angelo said.

"I think maybe we should try corn," Vincent said.

"I agree with Vincent. It's cheap to start off with but will make a good price," Anthony said.

"What do any of you know about corn?" Tristan asked.

"We know as much as you did about milking a cow when you came to Italy." Anthony smiled.

"Anthony is making fun of Tristan again. Ava, make him stop," Sophia said.

"Anthony stop before she has a cow," Ava said.

"I'm joking, babe," Anthony said.

"I know, but she will freak," Ava said.

"Are you OK, baby." Sophia sat on Tristan's lap.

"Yeah, our brother-in-law is just so moody." Tristan pointed.

"Ha! You are moody!" Sophia yelled.

"Oh my gosh! I am supposed to believe everything he says because Tristan pointed at something."

"You boys argue like children," Maria said.

"We all want and need the same things, to work together. We all have families that need to get fed and to survive this winter," Vincent said.

"And we all are going to do whatever it takes to make sure that happens, whether it's corn or wheat or whatever, right, everybody?" Bella said. "It ain't just one by one anymore; it's all for one and one for all."

"Right, no matter what, we will always be a family, and stay a family." Ava smiled.

"I married the smartest woman alive," Vincent said.

"Oh my gosh, Gina, don't put that in your mouth," Ava said.

"Tristan, will you...can you even try to get your son to sleep?" Maria said, handing Christian over.

"Rosa, go to Daddy while I help clean," Bella said.

Vincent took Rosa happily and began trying to get her to sleep, while still talking with the brothers about riding into town to buy wheat or corn. Or if the rain permitted, maybe they could plant vineyards. Who knew within a year they would all be one big, happy family arguing, with babies and wives and husbands of their very own?

The argument was almost like music to their ears, or something that they had just gotten used to anyway. A family, altogether, all the time. Always there when you need them to argue, always there when you need them to listen. The work, the prayer, the sacrifice. Sometimes you never know what you have until...it's gone.

SUMMARY

WE HAVE ALL HEARD IT SAID, "YOU CAN PICK YOUR FRIENDS, BUT you cannot pick your family."

I would have never picked another family than the one I have.

That saying is amazing and incredible to say the least, because there are many times in life, your family gets on your nerves. They may rattle every nerve in your body, but in the end, they are the ones who matter; they know what love is all about. They know what makes you happy not just the greeting on your face but the smile in your heart.

Take the time to know them, be friends with them, be loud with them, and be loyal to them.

Talk over each other, laugh with each other, cry with each other, and learn with each other.

Protect each other, amaze each other, and build from each other.

Share memories with your siblings, grow up together, and grow old together. Nobody is anymore the same than you, nor ever shall be.

Love them while they are here. Appreciate every single thing about them, from the way they laugh to the way they cry, because no other person is exactly like them.

God gave them to you to love, laugh with, and listen to. There is nobody better to love you and have your childhood memories with than your family.

ACKNOWLEDGMENTS

THIS BOOK IS DEDICATED TO MY FAMILY: MAMA, SHIRLEY JOANN Garlen; Daddy, Roby Garlen Jr.; my sister, Melissa (Mickey) Garlen Duke; Larry Duke; and my boys, Adam Duke, Sidney Duke, and Sawyer Duke, who were always more like my brothers than nephews. I am grateful for every smile they ever put on my face, every hug they ever gave, and every tear they ever dried and for every return text or call that said, "I love you too," "Happy Birthday," or "I'm so proud of you." Ya'll made my life growing up a safe and happy place, and you still are making my life a happy place right now. Every day is a little brighter because of you. My love and loyalty to you always.

Also to Lindsey Chawbowski Duke, who can do anything she sets her mind to; all my nephews and nieces; and my amazing children, Taylor Joanna Wilson and Kell Wilson, and (Olivia Williams) whom God gave to me as miracle children.

All my encouragement and kind words. This just keeps getting better. Thank you, Lord.

Thank you to Kelly Dittoe, and Katie Dahm-Johnson for being such a pleasure to work with and a blessing in my life.

Last but not least, thank you to Mr. Ferdia-Walsh Peelo, and Mr. Mark Mckenna.

ABOUT THE AUTHOR

MY NAME IS ADRIENNE GARLEN. I AM FORTY-FOUR YEARS OLD. I have two wonderful children: Taylor Joanna Wilson and Kell Patrick Wilson.

I developed a passion for stories and ideas when I was very young. It wasn't until I was older that I thought maybe I could possibly do something about it. I shared stories or poems I had written in school with my friends, and then from about 1996 until this past year, I came to a standstill. My writing suddenly came back, and there was no stopping it. I was able to travel everywhere in my mind through every story I wrote. It was so unbelievable, to say the least!

I am so thankful for this time in my life and for the Writers Lift on Twitter.

CPSIA information can be obtained
at www.ICGtesting.com
Printed in the USA
LVHW051945240122
709218LV00019B/1423